The Unpredictable

Written By

Elina Salajeva

Created By

Elinadeivid

DISCLAIMER

This is a work of fiction. Names, characters, businesses, places, events and incidents are either the products of the author's imagination or used in a fictitious manner. Any resemblance to actual persons, living or dead, or actual events is purely coincidental.

The right of Elina Salajeva, Elinadeivid to be identified as the author & creator of the work has been asserted by her & him in accordance with the Copyright, Designs and Patents Act 1988.

DEDICATION

To Deivid who has been a source of great inspiration and support over the years.

ACKNOWLEDGMENTS

Touchladybirdlucky Studios
A David Gomadza Production

PROLOG

One hundred years ago the magnificent seven girls were born to protect the young Emperor by the name of Nick in the United States of America. [The Girl With The Tiger Tattoo And The Magnificent Six by Elina Salajeva]. No one knows what happened to them. Over the past decades no information about what had happened to them existed. No one knows if the magnificent seven ever managed to protect the Emperor and preserve his bloodline. Is there another Emperor whose life and bloodline is worth preserving? It has been one hundred years now since the days of the magnificent seven girls.

CHAPTER ONE

"Sir, the monitors are registering an entity on earth and it's a few minutes before we close the gates. What shall we do? We never left anyone behind," said the man in the big oval office looking at the large screen in front of him. The other man walked toward the big screen and stopped. A beeping sound can be heard coming from the screen and a flashing beacon is seen on the screen.

"How is that possible?" asked the man touching the screen. He zoomed where the flashing beacon was.

"Everyone knows they should not stay on

earth during the night what is that person still doing there?" asked the man not expecting an answer.

"Honestly, I do not know, sir. I guess another causality."

"We can't risk going back there. We do not have time. Remember what happened to Adam and his men? We do not want that to happen again," said Sylvester the man in charge at the gate. Before he even finished talking, an automated voice was heard.

"Initiating gate closure. Loading parameters... Searching for human life still on earth." The automated voice stopped, and the beeping started. The machine went on for some seconds before a red beacon light started flashing followed by a siren.

"Problems detected! Still, human life on earth. Please confirm now. Continue or Abort. You have sixty seconds." As soon as the automated voice stopped a countdown began.

"59, 58, 57, 56, 55..."

"Sir what should I do?" asked Jaden. Sylvester stayed silent thinking about what to do. He had a split decision to make.

"Sir, can I abort or continue with the gate closure?" asked Jaden again this time hysterically. Sylvester couldn't answer straight away. This was a tough decision for him to make too.

"Ten seconds to go!" shouted Jaden looking at his boss who seemed lost for a while. "9, 8, 7, 6, 5...." An automated female voice can be heard counting down. Sylvester took his hand and wiped the sweat coming down his forehead.

"Continue with gate closure," said Sylvester.

"Are you sure Sir?" asked Jaden with his finger on the enter button on the screen. He looked at his boss who in turn nodded his head in agreement. There were two seconds left the time Jaden pressed the continue button on the screen.

'Gate closure initiated at 23:00 hours.' The image on the screen was that of the gate showing the closure on the screen. Jaden looked at his boss who was sweating. He looked at the screen as an alert message was displayed.

"Human life detected on earth at 23:00 hrs. Are you sure you want to proceed?" asked the automated voice on the screen. The screen this time turns to red while flashing.

"Please confirm closure or abort the operation now," said the automated female voice from the computer screen. Sylvester took a handkerchief from his suit pocket and wiped the sweat on his forehead before acknowledging to Jaden to continue with the gate closure.

"30, 29, 28, 27, 26, 25...."

The automated voice started the countdown to the gate closure. Both man in the gate office looked at each other before looking at the flashing screen especially at the red beacon standing for the person left behind.

"Gate successfully closed at 23:05 hrs. Possible one human causality," said the female automated voice. Both man looked at each other speechless. Jack is standing near the lake. He has been standing there for some time now. The lake is blue resembling the blue skies above. Golden-orange clouds are scattered in the sky. A cool breeze is blowing circulating the contours of the valley that encompass the lake. Jack has been visiting this lake for more than he remembers. Since he turned eighteen for unknown reasons, he had found himself at this lake. He has flashbacks of having been there before when he was about seven years old. He finds peace and somehow feels very connected to this lake. There is one huge boulder in the lake that is submerged into the water. Looks very shiny from afar. The boulder that has fascinated him is the second boulder that floats on top of the lake next to the submerged water. This is a huge boulder that has tended to beat gravity. It is a very beautiful boulder that has a rusty-blue green color. Very beautiful mountains surround the lake. Jack has some flashbacks of the time he had been here. He was a little boy. He still remembers how the water in the lake felt. The water was very warm and he could not explain it. He looks straight ahead to the mountains far away. He can see some smoke coming out from one of the mountains. Could that be a volcano? That could explain everything, Jack thought to himself. The day he remembers being at the lake as a kid could, the volcano had erupted causing the warm temperatures in the lake. That could also explain the dead fish and the dead marine wildlife he saw the other day. Jack stood there for some time. He was trying to put the pieces together. Possible the warm water had killed the fish. Or the volcano erupted some gasses that killed the marine life. Was the gas responsible also for his disorientation that day? He felt dizzy and could not remember what happened that day. It was eleven years ago when he first arrived here but he can still remember it like yesterday. He remembered waking up after hearing a big bang and the flashing of water. He remembered swimming out of the lake. He remembered the smell of the dead fried fish as he swam out of the lake waters. Ever since he had not been in the lake waters. He still has some fears. He cannot understand why but he loves coming here. He remembered the day he arrived there were no boulders in the lake that were submerged. He can't explain why now there are two big boulders in the lake. Tomorrow 25th of December is his birthday. This day 24th of December coincided with the first day he arrived here eleven years ago. Every time he comes to this place he sleeps standing, he goes into a trance-like state. When he wakes up, he feels more invigorated and energetic as if he has been recharged. It's more than forty-five minutes since he had been standing beside the lake. For the first time in years he stepped into the lake water. He stopped for a few seconds. The lake water was cold. He looked down in the water and at that moment he saw the image of the boulder moving. He stepped backward quickly in shock and looked at the floating boulder. Somehow the boulder had moved, and it seemed it was now facing the other way. He shook his body as a cold shiver goes up his spine. He waited a minute as he felt a warm feeling on his tattoo which is located on his back shoulder. He felt his body temperature rising starting from the legs. He looked at the boulder as he entered the lake waters again. He stopped and looked very carefully at the floating boulder above the lake waters. Nothing happened. Somehow, this time he did not feel the coldness of the water. Slowly he entered the lake water. As soon as his body was in the water, and as soon as the water came into contact with his tattoo on his back. The boulder started floating in the air away from him and toward the other boulder in the lake. He stopped and looked around him. The boulder stopped floating too. He started swimming toward the boulder. The boulder started floating again toward the other boulder. The boulder reached above the other boulder and flipped ninety degrees to the right. Jack felt a hot sensation on his tattoo that he quickly touched it. As soon as he had touched his tattoo the boulder already in the water flipped one hundred and eighty degrees facing upwards. Water splashed everywhere covering Jack who used his hands to wipe his face. As soon as he has touched his eyes, the boulders joined together. The floating boulder sat on top of the submerged boulder.

"Damn! It is a spaceship." Shouted Jack to himself. He remembered the day he arrived. He was in a spaceship. So, the spaceship landed in the water killing all the fish and rising the lake water temperature. Jack quickly moved toward the spaceship. He arrived at the spaceship but nothing happened. The door did not open as he had expected. He circled the spaceship looking for ways of opening the door. He looked at the door and saw a sign. He stopped and thought for a while. He remembered having a stone with the same sign years ago. He touched the spaceship but nothing happened. He touched his tattoo and a flash of light quickly runs through the middle line of the joined spaceship. Suddenly the top spaceship separated from the submerged spaceship. The other spaceship slowly goes above the lake water and drifted to its original position and stopped. Jack quickly swam out of the lake water. As soon as his legs were out of the lake water, the spaceship flipped ninety degrees anticlockwise. It soon camouflaged itself to a rusty- blue-green color. Jack looked at the ship for a while and started going toward his car. He touched his tattoo and his clothes started drying up and his body temperature adjusting accordingly. The door to his car opened and auto-start started the car. A few minutes later he was in his car ready to go home. He waited for a while looking at the ship in the lake before driving off. He headed to the gate in the city. A century after the days of the girl with the tiger tattoo and the magnificent six, earth had changed dramatically. The ozone layer had been destroyed and temperatures on earth at night would fall dramatically to minus fifty degrees Celsius. This meant that most people could not sleep and survive the night temperatures. Earth was now inhabitable at night. Since the destruction of the ozone layer high above the skies another layer of gaseous membrane had formed and solidified meters above the ground. The scientist had discovered that through certain areas people can pass through the membrane and live on this membrane above earth. This acted in the same way as the earth ground. People could build a shelter on the solidified membrane above earth. During the day, you could not stay there as temperatures of the sun would potentially cook you alive. There was the risk caused by the harmful ultraviolet rays emitted by the sun. The membrane was acting as the new ozone layer protecting the earth from the sun's radiation during the day. This formed when the ozone layer above the skies was destroyed by harmful gasses. The new membrane acted as the new protector of the earth from radiation above. The scientist had manipulated this and at night the membrane would protect the people from the freezing temperatures on the ground. During the day, this membrane would protect people from the sun's radiation above. This meant staying on earth during the day and traveling up at night to sleep. Scientists had discovered that at some points on earth it is easy to penetrate the membrane. It was possible to pass through to the other side. These points were called as the membrane gates or just the city gates. While driving to the city gate, Jack remembered the day he first arrived here eleven years ago. He remembered nearly dying of cold that night. He remembered leaving the warm waters of the lake and wandering toward the city. He was not scared, he remembered looking forward to meeting someone. Over the years, he had forgotten whom he was going to meet that night. He remembered feeling very excited that day. The nightmare began when he reached the city. It was night time by the time he arrived. No one was in the city. He did not even see anyone. Fear crippled him. Where were all the people? What had happened to humankind? He could not understand why there was no one in the city. The city was like a ghost town. The only difference being that lights were on. This meant that people were still around. He remembered shouting and screaming for help. He remembered feeling very cold as temperatures plunged to minus degree within minutes. It was that cold that he thought he was going to die of cold.

"Hello! Anyone! Help me! Where are you?! Please I need help." Screamed Jack as he arrived at the city hotel. No one seemed to have been there. He walked to the residential areas and to his surprise no one was there too.

"Hello please help. Anyone home!" shouted Jack looking for help. All the homes were deserted. He broke into one of the houses in the nearby suburban areas. He switched the lights and the heaters on. After an hour or so the lights and the heaters stopped working. Jack looked for anything he can put on and use to cover himself to feel warm. At one point, he felt going into a trance. It was that cold that his body activity was shutting down. It was after this that he felt a sharp pain coming from his back shoulder. He touched the tattoo on his shoulder with his right hand and suddenly his body temperature suddenly started going up. Jack looked at his watch. A flashing message was being displayed on the watch screen.

"You have less than 3 hours left of battery life. Please switch to auto power save or find an alternative power source.". Jack quickly looked at his watch. He stood up and looked for warm clothes. He looked at the watch again as it started flashing again.

"You have not eaten in more than five hours. Your energy reserves are running low. Please top up now."

Read the message on his watch. Jack scrolled down the screen options and selected this option.

"Initiate artificial refueling,"

"Impossible your reserves are empty," read the message on his watch. Jack quickly scrolled down the options again and selected another choice.

"Subjugate others with task and leech afterwards," The watch responded quickly.

"Wait, a moment... searching for other entities to subjugate" Jack waited impatiently as his watch searched for other people in the vicinity.

"Come on come on." Shouted Jack.

"There must be someone on earth. At least one whom I can use."

"Sorry. There are no other entities found on earth. Subjugating aborted."

"Damn! I am going to die here! I have to go back to the ship," shouted Jack. He quickly gathered what he can and left the house he had broken into. He walked and sometimes ran making his way back to the ship. He kept looking at his watch. It was only a few hours but ice was everywhere. His greatest fear was that the lake waters would be frozen making it hard for him to get into the ship. After two and half hours he was at the lake. Luckily the water was not frozen yet. This was partly because when he landed, the ship changed the water temperature and a lot of heat and energy was kept underneath the lake. Jack opened the ship door with a stone-like key he had. As soon as he entered the ship he fell into a trance. Half way through the night Jack was woken up by an automated voice from the ship.

"Subjugating successful hunger temporarily shifted to a one Adonis."

"Adonis? Who is Adonis? Where is this Adonis? I thought that no one else was on earth," said Jack talking to himself. Jack quickly scrolled down his watch. He searched the location of this Adonis. The watch displayed the results.

"Location Unknown,"

"Unknown?" shouted Jack.

"How is that possible? How did this system manage to locate him in the first place?" He quickly typed something on the ship's computer. An automated startles everyone.

"Initiating searches for a one Adonis."

A few seconds later an automated female voice is heard saying.

"Location Unknown. Definitely not earth." Jack kept thinking about this all night. In the office at the gate Jaden and Sylvester are woken up by an automated female voice.

"A human entity on earth can no longer be detected," and the screen was all green. The red beacon that was on the screen had disappeared. They both looked at each other.

"Tomorrow asks the engineers to have a look at this and all the infrared cameras." Said Sylvester feeling much relieved.
"Possibly he or she is dead now Sir," said Jaden fearing the worst.
"Dead no. If he or she had died, the computer will still be able to detect him or her. Possibly this was nothing after all." The two men after that slept like there is no tomorrow. Both relieved that no one had died. This all happened eleven years ago.

CHAPTER TWO

Moscow, Russia eleven years ago, 24th of December one hundred years after the girl with the tiger tattoo and the magnificent six. Ashley was shopping with his wife Princess' in Moscow City on Christmas eve. Ashley was too busy with work that they did not find time to shop early for Christmas as they normally did all these years. They had gone with their daughter Emma. This was the first time the family had been together for weeks. Moscow was magical during the Christmas festive. There were a lot of family activities in the city center. There were unique art objects paraded in the streets. There were a lot of street shows and concerts too. There were a lot of shops selling traditional food and unusual souvenirs. The family had been to the city square where there was a big Christmas ball highly decorated with led-lights. Just after the Manezh square in the city they had seen a big Christmas tree. This was the best time for the family.

"Daddy, look at the Christmas tree. It's beautiful and very decorated. Next year can we have one that big for us?" asked Emma holding her daddy's hand. Ashley and Princess both laughed and looked at their daughter.

"We will try but the tree is too big for our house," said Princess.

"We can put the tree outside our house mummy," exclaimed Emma seriously.

"Ok my princess we will do that next year. Ok?" said Ashley.

"Ok daddy thanks," said Emma.

"Ah that is my girl," said Ashley rubbing Emma's hair. They had been to the square when they came across a woman selling hot dogs. They stopped and bought hot dogs. They started walking in the park heading toward the market entrance.

"Mummy I left my doll. I will go and get it now." said Emma running back to the park bench where they were seated before.

"No Emma wait. Let's go there together.", Said Princess but Emma had already gone. Princess was looking at Emma as she sped off running back to the park bench. She turned to look at her husband Ashley only to find him on the ground with blood coming out of his body. He could not speak.

"Ashley! Ashley! What happened to you Darling!?" Princess knelt down before hearing a buzz sound passing her ears as if a sound made by a bee. When Emma came back, she found her parents on the ground.

"Mummy, Daddy! Mummy!" shouted Emma as she hugged both her parents. A car screeched its wheels to a halt meters away from the family. Emma raised her head and saw the window of the car opening slowly. Somehow, she quickly looked at her watch which was flashing. There was a message on the screen. She looked at the car again and quickly scrolled down her watch.

"You have five seconds to subjugate. Press Enter Now!" read the message on her watch. She looked at the car again and saw something pointing at her. She tried to get up and ran but her watch beeped.

"Searching for an entity to subjugate," "Come on hurry up," She raised her head again and saw a gun pointed at her. Fear crippled her. For a second or so she just looked at the car. It was the beep that drew her attention. 'Jadanick located. Press enter to subjugate Jadanick.' Quickly she pressed the enter option and at the same time she felt the most excruciating pain. She lay there on the ground looking in the skies. For some reason, she realized that God was just showing off when he created the stars. The sky looked very beautiful to her. She heard the car speeding off as she lay on the ground. In Hollywood, United States of America Jadanick, on Christmas eve was with his friends shopping. This was also the day before his birthday. Shopping was great. They had been everywhere in the city. The local rivals had just turned up in their car bragging and showing off. The people gathered to see what was going on. After a few minutes Jadanick screamed and fell to the ground. "Call an ambulance he has been shot. Help! Call for help. Now!" screamed one of Jadanick's friends. Jadanick was bleeding badly by the time the ambulance arrived. No one knew who had shot him but it was obvious it could have been one of the rival members.

"Who shot me man?" asked Jadanick looking at Noel.

"Do not talk Jadanick you are going to be OK." The ambulance arrived at the hospital and Jadanick was rushed to the operating room.

"What do we have here?" asked the doctor. "Possibly a gunshot wound. A lot of blood loss." Replied the senior nurse. The doctor and the nurses worked very fast and quickly removed the bullet fragments and stopped the bleeding. Blood transfusion was carried out after the operation. Hours later, Jadanick was declared as in a stable condition. Ever since the gunshot Jadanick had realized that life is too short. He nearly lost his life at the tender age of seven years. Ever since he had not stopped chasing his dreams. Since that day in the hospital he made an oath that if he survives this ordeal, he was to start pursuing his dream as a musician. He had been in the school choir at junior grades. He loved music. He had become very famous in Hollywood especially after being shot. He was now very strong and popular. He still remembers clearly the day he was shot. Somehow, he felt as if he was being subdued. He felt weak before he felt the most excruciating pain and falling to the ground. He felt being weak first and then the pain followed. Eleven years after that incident, tonight is his big night. At the age of eighteen he has a recording contract already. He had released some songs already. Tonight, he will be performing in front of thousands. He had looked forward to this day for months now. He had been rehearsing in his studio.

"Darling tonight is your big night I just

want to let you know that I am very proud of you and I love you very much." Said Sandra putting her arms around Jadanick.

"Thanks babes I appreciate that" Jadanick replied kissing Sandra.

"Invite your friends as well Sandy let's make the night one to remember. Okay?" asked Jadanick.

"I already did Darling," replied Sandra. These two had been going out for a few months now and it was great. A few hours later the show had begun. Jadanick was a natural born singer. There was magic in his voice. The people loved him. All the girls loved him. It was his time. That gun wound had taught him a lesson; never to look back and to chase your dreams never giving up. The crowd stood up as he approached the stage and everyone went hysterical when he appeared on the stage. The atmosphere was magical. The arena was fully packed. Jadanick walked on the stage, grabbed the microphone and without saying anything to the crowd he started singing one of his favorite songs. The crowd started clapping hands, others whistling and women throwing whatever they can on the stage. Girls in front of the stage started screaming and dancing.

"Hello everyone! It's Jadanick here. I am honored to have you tonight. I hope you are going to enjoy the show as much as me. Wow!" Shouted Jadanick to the applause of the crowd. The concert began smoothly to everyone's delight. It was half way through the concert that Jadanick felt a strange feeling.

"Déjà vu," he screamed and stopped singing. He felt a strong sensation that he had experienced before what he was feeling.

"No! No! No! Not again."

Shouted Jadanick. The crowd went berserk, and they all started singing after him, "No! No! No! Not again."

"Darling what is wrong? Did you forget your lyrics" asked Sandra as she approached Jadanick who seemed a bit confused?

"I do not know I have this strange feeling. Maybe it's nothing," said Jadanick as he continued with the show. Three minutes

into the next song Jadanick was down.
"I got shot again. I knew it. Damn who shot me?" asked Jadanick as he lay on the stage floor. Emma has arrived in the United States of America from Moscow, Russia where she has been for the past eleven years. After her parents' death and her miraculously survival she has been in-hiding. At the age of eighteen years old she had traveled to the USA. After the second attempt on her life she had realized that if she must live, she must escape and head to America. She went to the gate in the city looking for Jadanick. On two separate occasions this Jadanick had saved her life. She had never met this Jadanick before but her watch on two separate occasions had assigned Jadanick to be the subjugating recipient. The one who experienced the pain she should instead have experienced.
"How can I help you, a young lady?" asked the gate attendant after noticing that Emma looked lost.
"I am looking for Jadanick," replied Emma
"There could be thousands of Jadanick's out there," replied the gate attendant.

"No! No! This one is a special friend. He isn't just Jadanick." replied Emma.

"Oh, is that so?" asked the gate attendant.

"We have not met before but I can tell if I see him," explained Emma.

"I will give you all the addresses of the Jadanick in this area." said the gate attendant before continuing.

"What does this Jadanick does if I may ask you?" asked the gate attendant.

"He protects the Emperor. He is an Imperial guard. He serves and honors the Emperor," said Emma. The gate attendant thought that she was joking and started laughing.

"Protects the Emperor is that so? Where is this Emperor?" asked the gate attendant Oska.

"That's my next task once I have found Jadanick." replied Emma.

"There are no Emperors nowadays. We have only Presidents and Prime Minister." Replied Oska.

"So where are you planning to find this Jadanick?" asked Oska.

"Honestly, I do not know I thought maybe

you might know you are security yes?" asked Emma.

"You can say that, but the only Jadanick I know is this one." said Oska taking out a poster of Jadanick from one of the music magazines.

"Yes, very funny," replied Emma.

"Why? He could be the Jadanick you are looking for." Said Oska jokingly.

"I am looking for an Imperial guard. One who guards the Emperor," replied Emma.

"So where is the Imperial Palace?" asked Emma going through the music magazine.

"Like I said there are no Emperors anymore," replied Oska.

"That can't be true. I am an Imperial bodyguard too just like Jadanick. We are born to serve, to protect and to honor the Emperor. There must be an Emperor's Palace somewhere nearby." Said Emma.

"What makes you say that?" asked Oska.

"I had a dream. This gate is situated at the former Imperial gate. One hundred years ago, the Emperors Palace was located here." said Emma expecting Oska to laugh at her.

"I guess you are right. I have read it somewhere in one of the brochures the days I started working here."
Acknowledged Oska.
"So, you know I am telling you the truth." Remarked Emma. Oska and Emma were busy talking when Emma collapsed and fell into a trance. Oska quickly called for help and moved her in the first aid room in the gate office waiting for help to arrive.

CHAPTER THREE

Jack arrived at the gate from the lake. It
was the 24th of December on Christmas
eve. He had remembered everything about
the key and the ship. It was now too late to
go back to the lake after all the following
day was his birthday and Christmas day as
well. He planned to look for the key and
return to the ship. He parked his car and
went into the lift taking him up to the
world above earth to sleep. Jack had just
arrived at the gate. He looked at his
flashing watch. A beeping sound was
activated, and a message was on the
screen, 'Unknown entity.' Jack looked

around as if looking for someone. He stood there for some time. He looked at his watch again. He scrolled down and entered search command. A beeping sound is released from the watch. A please wait searching in progress message is displayed on the screen.

"Come on. Who is out here?" said Jack talking to himself. Oska was watching Jack all this time. He approached Jack.

"Hello. Are you Jadanick by any chance?" asked Oska. Jack looked lost he raised his head and replied Oska.

"Eh, what? Who? Oh No?" replied Jack.

"Are you okay Sir?" asked Oska.

"Yes Sure," replied Jack. Jack looked at his watch before cursing.

"Damn an unknown entity again." He said it loud that Oska heard him.

"Do not worry I am fine," said Jack walking away from the gate office. Jack headed to the lake. He had found that stone that looked like the key to the ship. He was very excited. This was what he wanted to know. This was his mission. All his questions will be revealed to him once he is in the ship. This ship will take him to the Emperor. He started having flashbacks. He remembered coming here to look for someone. He remembered being very happy and excited about all this but he had forgotten who he was to meet. Over the past years, he had come to the understanding that he was an Emperor's bodyguard. That is all he knew. He did not know where the Emperor was. Soon he was in his car heading for the lake. He arrived at the lake and quickly entered the lake waters. As soon as his legs were in the water the ship started moving to align with the other submerged part in the lake. He touched his tattoo and the ship flip 90 degrees clockwise. He wiped the water on his eyes with his hands and the ship joined together. Quickly he swam toward the ship. He put his hand in his pocket and took out the small stone and put it in the grove on the door. Soon a blue light runs across the area where the ships had joined together in the middle. The ship rose few centimeters out of the lake waters. Jack jumped inside. Excitedly and curiously. As soon as he was inside all his memories of being in the ship came back. He remembered saying goodbyes to his parents and leaving them. He quickly went through the computer in the ship. Play last messages received, he requested on the command prompt.

"Hello Jack, welcome back."

An automated voice is heard coming from the computer. He remembered leaving his parents as a kid going on a lifetime mission to protect the Emperor. This was the destination of the Emperors Palace. The coordinates were one hundred percent correct. He does not understand why he ended up here in the first place. The last message is played on the computer screen. It shows him very excited that he was going to serve and to protect the Emperor. A few minutes before he fell into a trance the ship's computer system had acknowledged that he had arrived at the Emperor's Palace. He understood why all these past eleven years he had made this journey to the lake. This only left more questions than answers. Was this the last

Emperor's Palace? In a lake? Surely, he had the feeling that the Emperor's Palace was at the now gate. Every time he is there he feels connected to the Emperor. Jack is in the ship. He typed on the prompt command asking the ship to show him and reprogram the last coordinates. He remembered the ship crushing in the lake. Something might have gone wrong that he ended up in the lake. That was his destination per the coordinates it's only that his landing was not smooth. After sometime he realized that the coordinates were just for his safe landing otherwise that was not his destination. He looked everywhere in the ship for clues as to where he was going after he had landed. There was nothing pointing to that. He was now sure that his destination was the gate. The former Emperor's home. He took everything he needed and recharged himself before going back to the gate. 'Warning your original course has been diverted due to circumstances beyond our control. Wind patterns had diverted your landing path. Please wear protective equipment and prepare for a crash-landing.' Was an automated message flashing on the screen?

"Damn. Why everything never goes to plan?" shouted Adonis. He got up quickly and walked to the big screen in the ship.

"Damn. It's miles away from the lake? How is that possible?" screamed Adonis. He quickly sat on the ship's computer seat and started typing frantically.

"Too late to change the course now. This is your best possible landing site with minor injuries."

Was an automated female voice coming from the ship's navigation system?

"You have a fifty percent chance of survival if you crash land here than anywhere else." This was the automated message from the ship's navigation system.

"Are you crazy? Just fifty percent?" shouted Adonis running to put on his crash-landing gear. Quickly he got dressed up and wore his helmet.

"Ten minutes to impact" shouted the automated voice from the ship.

"Ten minutes only you must be kidding me!" shouted Adonis entering the crash-landing bubble. Five minutes down the line his watch started flashing.

"Risk of death and loss of limbs on impact subjugate now. Press enter now." Read the message on his watch.

"Damn it's that bad," said Adonis scrolling down his watch. He pressed enter as fast as he can. 'Please wait while searching is in progress.' Read the message on his watch screen. After a few seconds, there was a new message on his watch screen. 'Please choose and subjugate now before impact.' Adonis quickly looked at the screen of his watch.

"Unknown Entity and Jadanick" appeared on the screen. Quickly he thought to himself and chose Unknown Entity and waited.

'Sorry we are unable to locate an Unknown Entity please choose another.'

Adonis looked at the message on his watch.

"Damn what is the difference with deliberately killing someone?" asked Adonis feeling guilty that this was like murdering someone else. It was the female automated voice that made him choose Jadanick as the choice for subjugating.

"Five seconds to impact brace yourself" said the automated female voice. Adonis realized that he was in a tight spot. He was in a do or die situation. Quickly he chose Jadanick. He waited to hear if that has been confirmed.

"2 seconds to impact," a female voice is heard from the ship speakers. Adonis looked at his watch and the last thing he noticed and saw on the screen was a 'subjugating completed' message. Jadanick was in the studio rehearsing when he stopped and looked at Sandra with that look that says here we go again and why me? Sandra quickly rushed to the studio door and tried to open it.

"Open the door right now Darling. Open the door," shouted Sandra. Nick did not say anything. For a minute, he looked lost and puzzled as to how Sandra knew. He touched himself and looked if he was bleeding. He was okay. So, how did Sandra know what he was feeling? He looked at her and felt his heart moving with love. Surely, she was meant for him. She could tell just by looking at him. That really surprised him and gave him some sense of comfort. He wanted to play down the fears but Sandra kept knocking the door. He slowly walked toward the door but unsure if that was the correct thing to do. He had just released the inside lock when he was thrown back into the studio hitting the floor hard and fainting. Sandra quickly called for help to take him to the hospital. The ambulance came and quickly Jadanick was rushed to the hospital. He was put on a drip and the nurse took his temperature reading. He was rushed to the hospital where he was stabilized.

"Can tell us what happened to him?" asked the doctor looking at Sandra.

"Honestly I am not sure but I think he fell in the studio?" said Sandra.

"Really, I thought he was involved in an accident because of the injuries. It must have been a serious fall," Said the doctor.

"It was a bad fall. How is he doing?" asked Sandra.

"Surprisingly great. He recovered quickly in the last hour than we have expected. He is a fighter. I think this is the first time I have seen somehow with such injuries recover that fast," explained the doctor.

"That's good news that he will recover soon." Said Sandra.

"Is he a musician? You said he fell in the studio?" asked the doctor.

"Yes. It's Jadanick. He is popular." Replied Sandra.

"Is he the one who was here also with a gunshot wound?" asked the doctor. Sandra looked at the window and looked at Jadanick. It was a while before she replied.

"Yes, it's him. He had been through a lot" said Sandra feeling sorry for her man.

"Even then that was not the first time correct?" Asked the doctor. Sandra looked surprised. She had no idea Jadanick was shot before.

"Really? I did not know about that. He once told me that he was shot as a kid but I just thought he was trying to impress me." They were moments of silence before the doctor spoke.

"Welcome to the world of music. East coast versus West coast. These artists they kill each other for nothing. I guess being shot sells records. I understand he is one of the richest in show business." Said the doctor trying to comfort Sandra.

"I wish he can stop singing and just have a normal life. How many chances can you get in life?" said Sandra feeling unhappy and afraid of Jadanick's future.

"I guess he is lucky the best doctors are around." Said the doctor touching Sandra's shoulder.

"Thank you doctor for all the help," said Sandra.

"You are welcome if you need anything let me know. Okay." Said the doctor leaving Sandra standing outside Jadanick's hospital room. The next day Jadanick had nearly fully recovered that everyone concerned was astonished. It seemed sleeping made him heal fast. He had slept for more than ten hours. They all gathered to hear what he was going to say. They spoke to him and the doctor brought some kids from the pediatrician to sing for him.

"Did you get shot again," asked one cheeky kid from the group. They all started laughing even Jadanick saw the funny side of this.

"Not this time. I just tripped and fell," replied Jadanick. The doctor recommended him to stay for a few days more for observation. The second day after this Jadanick was about to be discharged from the hospital when the unthinkable happened. Everyone was there sitting outside his hospital room. As a rich musician, he had his own room with glass walls around it. They were all sat outside his room when he stood up and looked at Sandra. At first, she looked at him too and waved her hand before continuing talking to the doctor. He stayed standing looking at Sandra. A feeling of fear crippled Sandra and instantly she stood up and walked toward the door to his hospital room.

"Not again," she spoke loudly to herself but loud enough for the doctor to have heard it.

"What is the matter?" asked the doctor. The doctor stood up and started walking toward Jadanick's room. They both reached the door to his room and looked at him through the glass walls. He looked at them. For the first time, Sandra saw fear in Jadanick's face. Jadanick was a very well built man. Ever since he was shot as a kid he had looked after himself. He regularly trained as he had a gym room next to his studio. He had grown big, and he loved it. That he had performed on his tours without wearing shirts or t-shirts which all the ladies loved. He swerved backwards as if someone had punched him. He staggered backward and covered his head with his hands as if someone was beating him up. He soon found himself on the ground. He growled in pain. He looked through the window as if asking Sandra for help. Sandra was about to enter his room when the doctor blocked the door.

"Wait do not enter the room. It is not safe for you too," said the doctor. Confused about what to do Sandra waited there for a second thinking about what to do.

Jadanick stood up and tried to go out of the room but somehow it looked like someone dragged him back inside. He growled in pain and touched his mouth. He was bleeding. When Sandra saw this, she fought her way in the room and hugged Jadanick pinning him to the bed. She hugged him and cried like a baby. The doctor stood there speechless. Was it a demon or something else? Even him he was scared. After a few days, he had fully recovered, and the doctor recommended him to research and try to find out why this was happening to him. The doctor had told Jadanick to go to the church in case demons possessed him. Jadanick dismissed the idea as that would damage his reputation.

"Doc, I was attacked by people who are blackmailing me. You didn't see anything. Right?" The doctor accepted a check written for the pediatrician ward for his silence. The following days Jadanick stayed in his bedroom in case something bad happen to him but that seemed to be the last of the mis-happenings in his life. Even though he was happy after that he had this nagging feeling about all this.

Secretly he started researching about this. He befriended one of the private investigators money can buy by the name of Natasha to help him resolve this whole thing.

CHAPTER FOUR

Somewhere in Latvia, Riga city eleven years ago.

"Alina, Alina? Where are you? Come grandmother and grandfather are here to see you. They brought birthday and Christmas presents for you. Come now," shouted Alina's mother Carolina.

"Ok I am coming mummy." Replied Alina coming down from her bedroom upstairs.

"Oh, that is our granddaughter. Come Alina to your grandmother," said grandmother opening her arms to welcome her. Alina ran to her grandmother and hugged her.

"It's not just my birthday tomorrow it's Christmas as well grandmother," said Alina with her eyes wide opened.

"I know our granddaughter we have brought you a load of presents." Said grandfather sliding a big Santa Claus bag full of presents for Alina. She was very excited that she started dancing jumping up and down clapping her hands.

"Thank you, grandma, thank you grandpa," remarked Alina.

"Take the presents and put them under the Christmas tree and open them tomorrow Alina," asked Carolina.

"Ok mummy."

Quickly Alina took the presents out of the Santa clause bag and placed them under the Christmas tree.

"Tomorrow I am going to see my sister." Said Alina very happy. Everyone just thought that she was very happy and looking forward to Christmas and her birthday. The grandparents all stayed for Christmas. Christmas day came and Carolina went to her daughter's room to wish her a happy birthday and a merry

Christmas. She opened the door and shouted.

"Happy birthday Alina. You are seven years today. Wake up!" Carolina was clapping hands and singing. Alina was fast asleep. She was in a trance. She was breathing but could not wake up despite her mum's efforts to wake her up. They soon took her to the hospital. Nothing seemed wrong with her. She was in a deep sleep. Her eyebrows were moving, and she was breathing but she was not responding. Christmas day, her parents spend the day in hospital. Days came and gone with no sign of her waking up. It was on new years' day that Alina finally woke up. She talked about traveling to Russia to meet her sister. She talked about celebrating her birthday with her and having Christmas with her. She came back with a watch. She had insisted that her sister had given her this watch. Her parents had assumed that one of the nurses or doctors in the hospital had given her the watch the time she was in the hospital. She had a photo of her and her sister taken in Moscow Russia. She showed the photo to her parents. They didn't know what to believe.

"So, tell us about your sister in Russia," asked Trevor looking at his daughter who seemed more concerned about her watch than anything else.

"Daddy I was in Moscow with Emma. She had invited me back. It was both our birthdays, and it was Christmas time too," said Alina very excited jumping on the sofa and then sitting next to her father.

"This sister of yours did she ask about us?" asked Trevor brushing this story aside.

"Not really, she had told me before I left here that I was going there and never coming back to you," Alina paused for a while typing something on her watch.

"What never coming back home? Why? You are our daughter. How can you leave us and never come back?" asked Trevor. Alina did not reply straight away she was fiddling with her watch.

"I was supposed to go with her to our new family but I do not know why we didn't go, they can't find the Emperor something happened to him I guess. So, I came back.

She gave me this watch when the time comes she will let me know." Said Alina innocently. Trevor for some time looked confused. It all sounded genuine.

"So why the Emperor if I may ask?" asked Trevor curious.

"As you know I guard the Emperor and protect him for eternity," explained Alina speaking honestly.

"Oh, yes we know that," said Trevor jokingly.

"Did grandma bring you a toy of an Emperor or what?" asked Trevor looking at his daughter. Alina did not reply she was busy scrolling down on her watch. After a while she replied.

"A real Emperor dad," Trevor knew that was not possible.

"My sister said I will have a sign when I am ready to go. All I have to do is wear this watch never to remove it." Trevor looked bewildered but perplexed by all this. After this incidence, Alina had a tattoo on her shoulder. Trevor and Carolina believed her. The year when she was seven years old she waited in vain for the calling to start training. As she was clearly told by her sister initiation started at the age of seven. A year passed by without any major news from her sister. All she knew was that they can only initiate training when the Emperor was there. She thought that they had not found him yet. Eleven years down the line she had not given up hope. She communicated with her sister most of the time. She had traveled to Moscow to meet with Emma.

"So why we have not been called its eleven years now since the day we were supposed to start training to protect the Emperor," asked Alina.

"I think the Emperor is not in immediate danger or that he is not even born yet that could explain why we are still out here," explained Emma.

"Or we are no longer needed as the Emperor's bodyguards?" remarked Alina.

"Do not be silly we are the Emperor's bodyguards for eternity do not ever think that way." Said Emma comforting her sister Alina.

"You know why I said that? In one of my

trances I was told that last time they were all girls and probably this time they are all boys." Said Alina. Emma had never thought it that way. She felt she was one of the Emperor's guards to protect the Emperor. There was silence for some time. Alina realized that she might have said the truth. This was the only perfect reason why they had not left at the age of seven. "Do not forget the world has changed too. This daily shift between earth and the above world created problems for the Emperor as well." In the months leading to the month of December the girls kept falling in and out of trances. This was a sign of calling. The Emperor needed their assistance. It was snowing in Latvia just before Christmas. On the 24th of December at the age of eighteen years old Alina woke up in the middle of the night. She went into her parents' bedroom and stood there. There were both asleep. "It's time. I must go. I love you so much." She looked at her flashing watch. There was a message on the watch screen. 'You have ten minutes before your ship arrives.' Alina quickly closed the door behind her as she headed downstairs and out of the family house. She ran as fast as she can toward the nearby lake. She looked around but did not see the ship. She waited for some time, walked up and down the lake shores. It was then when she felt a burning sensation on her tattoo. She touched the tattoo on her back shoulder and the ship camouflage came off. She looked at the flashing watch. She took a small stone-like key from her pocket and moved toward the ship. She inserted the ship's key in the grove and the door opened. She jumped inside the ship. She just couldn't believe what she was seeing. It was beautiful inside with a lot of gadgets. She looked for the ship's manual but there was not any. While she was busy trying to find out how to operate the ship, a message appeared on the ship's screen. 'Auto- navigation commencing in 2 hours.' "You have reached your destination," a message was delivered through the ship's speakers and displayed on the ship's screen as well. Alina excitedly took the things she needed from the ship and opened the ship's door. The ship was above the lake waters. She jumped out into the lake waters and swam to land. The ship's door closed and the ship split into two. She watched the two separate halves camouflaged to look like rocks as they submerged into the lake water. She felt a warm sensation coming from her tattoo on her back shoulder and placed her hand there. Soon her body temperature started to adjust accordingly.

'Proceed to the gate,' message is displayed on her watch. Quickly she started making her way to the city's gate. Alina stood after a few meters and looked at her watch. There was a flashing message again being displayed. She looked at the message.

'Your visibility mode is currently on for your own safety switch to hide mode.' She scrolled down her watch and switch to hide mode. She got a lift and proceeded to the gate.

"Hello can you please tell me where I can find the Emperor?" asked Alina.

"Excuse me?" asked the gate office

attendant.

"Yes. I am looking for the Emperor or his place of residents."

"There are no Emperors anymore," replied Matthew "But I thought this was the Emperor's residents or somewhere around here," said Alina.

"Oh, yes, but a century ago," remarked Matthew.

"How can that be? There must be something. I have the feeling that the Emperor is here somewhere. In my trance, it's exactly this place I should be," said Alina talking to herself. She scrolled down her watch. She turned visibility mode on to search for the other Emperor's bodyguards. After a few seconds a message appeared on the screen.

'Unknown entity identified,".

"Yes," shouted Alina as she scrolled down her watch. She typed a message asking for the location of the entity and pressed the search button. A few seconds later a message is displayed on the watch.

'Location unknown.'

"Now what?" shouted Alina. She paused

for a while and quickly scrolled down her watch. She pressed the enter button on her watch. She waited for the results to be displayed. Soon after a message is displayed on the watch screen.

'Subjugating failed. Cannot connect to the entity.'

"Damn! What am I going to do?" asked Alina thinking loud. Alina went back to the gate office and spoke to Matthew.

"So, what happened to the Emperor's residence?" asked Alina. Matthew was busy checking something on the monitors and cameras in the gate office.

"Honestly I do not know much about that but what I heard is that the place had been abandoned for years when this place was acquired for the new development." Said Matthew.

"Do you know what happened to the Emperor or people who lived there?" asked Alina.

"I do not know much but there are a lot of e-books in the library about that I guess," responded Matthew.

"But you will need permission to enter the

library which you can get after a day or two," added Matthew.

"Ok get the permission for me I will use the library tomorrow. Right now, I just need to go and find the Emperor," replied Alina. Matthew just looked at her with that look that asks what Emperor? Alina was tired she sat in the gate office and started dozing off. It was the beeping sound from her watch that woke her up.

'Subjugating subject identified. Confirm to proceed,' she looked at her watch. She paused for a while thinking. Quickly she scrolled down and Jadanick. You have 5 seconds to subjugate before path disappears'. Quickly Alina scrolled down her watch. She chooses the abort subjugating option and instead selected the link and synchronize option and pressed enter.

'Linking…. please wait,' a message is displayed on the watch screen. She waited for a few seconds before the linking together was confirmed as successful. Another message popped up the screen. 'Synchronizing.. please wait,' a message appeared on the watch screen. Alina waited patiently before she cursed. "Damn!" she shouted in despair. The synchronizing failed message appeared on the screen. There was not enough time to synchronize the two. Jadanick was no longer in the vicinity. There was hope now that she could find someone who can help her understand all this. As long as Jadanick was nearby she could be able to trace and link with him if he does not reset his system. It was now getting dark and earth started getting cold. People were starting to leave earth as night was falling. Through the several gates the people started making their way to the above world leaving earth. Alina started searching for others using her watch. She waited at the gate hoping that someone will come through their going to the world above to sleep. She had been dozing off when she heard a beep sound from her watch. She looked at the watch. A synchronizing completed message appeared on the screen. She remembered trying to get synchronized to Jadanick but then again, a strange feeling struck her. Quickly she sat straight and scrolled on her watch. She searched the last operations performed on her watch. She discovered that she had been linked and synchronized to someone and that person was coming her way. Quickly she requested the identity of the person she has been synchronized to.

'Unidentified entity,' a message appeared on the screen. She sat there for some time thinking.

"What if it's an enemy then I will be at risk and more vulnerable because the person can subjugate and weaken me?" Alina was thinking loudly. She quickly got up and joined those who were making their way to the world on above level. Her watch was flashing, she quickly looked at the message on the screen.

'Unknown entity approaching. You might be at risk initiate subjugating now.' Alina looked at the message and fear struck her. She had a few seconds to think. There was no point to subjugate now. Quickly she switched off the watch and removed it from the wrist. She looked for the special container of the watch with functions to go invisible and jam infrared rays. Quickly she opened her small bag and placed the watch inside the special container. She then mingled with the rest of the people. After a while a big man with blonde hair was passing by where she was before he stopped. He looked at his watch, looked around and raised his arm as if to get better reception and entered the gate office. He went inside and looked at his watch again. Alina looked at him and to her surprise he did exactly like what she had done when she was inside the gate office. That freaked her. He went straight to sit exactly where Alina was sat. He stood up as he had done before and traced all the movements she had made. Even a time when she had mistakenly dropped her item and picked it up from the floor. It was at this point she realized what was going to happen next. Quickly she started going upwards going between the people who were in the queues. She was now at the top when she looked downwards. That man had taken her old place where she disconnected her watch. He looked up, and she looked away for a while. She looked down again, and the man was gone. It seemed he had lost the trail. That nearly crippled her with fear. He didn't look friendly. Definitely. He was not one of them. As far as she knew Emperor's bodyguards at one time could either be all girls or all boys. She knew there was Emma so technically they all could be girls. Quickly she found accommodation for the night in one of the hotels in the world above.

CHAPTER FIVE

Emma when she finally came around she found herself in the hospital.

"Where am I?" asked Emma. One of the nurses replied.

"You are in the private hospital. Don't you worry everything is going to be fine," replied the nurse.

"How did I get here? I remember...," said Emma without finishing her sentence.

"Yes. You have been transferred here after you didn't come around. I understand you fainted at the gate office," replied the nurse.

"This hospital looks luxurious. Who pays

for the bills?" asked Emma not expecting the nurse to answer.

"You. Pay for the bills," replied the nurse.

"Me?! What. Where can I get such money? I just arrived a few days ago." Replied Emma.

"Do not worry young lady. The bill has been paid already in advance," replied the nurse.

"By who? Did the Emperor pay for the bill?" asked Emma quickly getting out of the hospital bed. She didn't wait for the nurse to reply her.

"How did he find me? Where is he. Tell me I have to go there right now," quickly Emma started picking up her things as she talked?

"So where is the Emperor? I have to go there straight away," asked Emma staring at the nurse. The nurse stood there for some time not knowing what to say.

"Emperor? Where is he? The one who paid the bill. You know?" asked Emma expecting to be given an address. The nurse looked at Emma first before she replied.

"We saw a message on your watch asking us to subjugate Jadanick," she paused for a while looking at Emma before she continued.

"Who?" asked Emma.

"Jadanick. You know. The singer. Right?" explained the nurse.

"We contacted Jadanick and told him that you requested us to ask him to pay for the medical bill. To our surprise, he did not deny instead he asked you be given a private room and special medical attention," said the nurse.

"The only person who can to that is the Emperor or someone related to the Emperor," said Emma not expecting a reply from the nurse.

"This Jadanick is he a singer for the Emperor? Is he related to the Emperor? Does he work for the Emperor?" asked Emma.

"Honestly, I do not know why not go and talk to him yourself?" asked the nurse. The nurse took out an iPad and looked for an address. Is your bluetooth or infrared on I will send the address to your watch. Emma without replying looked at her watch and started scrolling down. It was after a few seconds before she acknowledged. A beeping sound is heard as she received the address on her watch. She scrolled for direction and engaged navigation system. "Ok, thank you very much," said Emma leaving the hospital. Emma after leaving the hospital headed straight to see Jadanick. She was excited at least this person knows something about the Emperor, she thought to herself. After all the mishaps that had happened to Jadanick he had taken security seriously. He had bodyguards as well as he was rich and a popular musician. He had a big mansion in Hollywood. Ever since that last incident Jadanick had been very not trusting people. It was like any other day in his life rehearsing his music or just chilling with his girlfriend Sandra and his friends.

"Boss there is a lady at the gate to see you," said Jadanick's bodyguard.

"Send her away I am not expecting anyone," replied Jadanick rehearsing in the studio.

"I tried Boss, but she insisted to meet you she said you paid for her hospital bill," replied the bodyguard.

"Oh. Yes. Tell her that it was a goodwill gesture," replied Jadanick leaving the studio and entering the living room to get something to drink. The bodyguard left and came back again.

"Boss the lady outside is asking if you are the Emperor or know the Emperor. She said she is a bodyguard of the Emperor and she is looking for the Emperor," said the bodyguard. Jadanick spit out the drink that was in his mouth when he heard this. He started laughing echoed by his friends.

"Tell her that it just depends with who wants to know. I can be her Emperor if she wants," said Jadanick. They all burst into laughter.

"Darling let me go and talk to this lady. Ok?" asked Sandra.

"Ok honey," replied Jadanick. Jadanick for some unexplained reason he had a strange feeling about this. He had been through his share of bad luck, all he wanted was to enjoy his riches and life. Another mishap surely can destroy him. Sandra came back with Emma.

"Darling meet Emma. Emma this is Jadanick," said Sandra. The two came face to face, and all screamed before both fainted. They both fell on the ground touching their chests. They both were in an out of unconsciousness. They re-lived the day they were both shot. Jadanick acted exactly like the day he was first shot as a kid. Sandra ordered the bodyguards to put Jadanick in his bedroom and Emma was put in the guest room. The following morning Jadanick went into the kitchen looking for something to drink. He looked first to see if Emma was inside before entering the kitchen. He opened the fridge door and took something to drink. He was about to drink when Emma entered the kitchen. He looked at her, their eyes came face to face and they both saw and re- lived the second time they were shot. They fainted again. The bodyguards rushed to their rescue. Jadanick knew this time what was going on. Somehow Emma was involved in his shootings, on both occasions. When he looked at her on both occasions he re-lived the days, he was shot. First when he was seven years old on Christmas eve and when he was seventeen years old. He recalled that there was another incident when he crash-landed in the studio. He sat on the couch first before inviting Emma in the lounge area. The pain he experienced that day in the studio made him squint but somehow, he knew she had the answers to his questions. Emma entered the lounge area and stopped hoping to experience pain or something but nothing happened. They both kept in their positions Jadanick was holding onto the couch in case he is thrown forceful downwards. Minutes passed but nothing happened.

"So, the crash- landing, wasn't you? How many of you are out there? You nearly got me killed? You got me shot! Why?" asked Jadanick. Emma surprised sat down and looked at Jadanick in disbelieve.

"Are you the Emperor? That can't be right! Something is wrong. Where is the

Emperor?" asked Emma not expecting answers anywhere from Jadanick.

"Hell no! Emperor? Me? No way. Who told you that? Is that why you got me shot? Who are you?" asked Jadanick. There was a moment of silence before Emma replied.

"I am an Emperor's bodyguard." Jadanick interrupted.

"What Emperor bodyguard? My fat belly," exclaimed Jadanick. In a soft voice, Emma responded.

"A minute ago, you said that I got you shot. So, how did I do that?". Jadanick knew she was right.

"Ok, tell me what are you doing here? This is not China? You want an Emperor then go to China. What does this have to do with me? And how did you manage to get me shot?" Asked Jadanick putting the macho vibes down. He really wanted to know how that happened.

"Somehow you and me we are linked, we are connected, we all serve the Emperor somehow," said Emma.

"Wait a minute, hold on, stop this kind of talk. I do not serve anyone. I am the

Emperor myself. I am not part of this. You mean I am your bullet bag I just take bullets for you. Is this how I am to you. You got me shot not just once but twice. So clearly, we are not in the same team. I nearly died. Look at these scars you think this is a joke?" asked Jadanick showing Emma the bullet scars on his body. Emma started crying.

"My parents were killed on Christmas eve," she stopped talking and cried for a while.

"That same night, I was shot too but just before I subjugated you as the recipient," she paused and looked at Jadanick who remained sat and speechless.

"I am very sorry to hear about your parents," said Jadanick.

"I had gone back to collect my doll from the park bench when it happened. When I came back, there was blood everywhere. So much blood even now I can still see it. Dad was already dead. Mum was still alive. When she saw me, she wanted me to run away, but I just stood there for a while before hugging her. That is when that car approached. It was like in slow motion. I saw the window of the car being opened and a gun being pointed at me. I had only 5 seconds to react. I had no chance of surviving. The system calculated that you had better chances of surviving if you took the bullets. I had seconds to save myself. When I saw your name on the radar, honestly, I can't tell you how I felt. I had hopes of surviving. Only you kept appearing as my subjugating target. I am here today because of you. You are my hero, you saved me, not just once but twice. Now thrice by paying my hospital bill. So now you see why I said we are linked. I do not know your role but we are all together. Maybe you just do not know it." There was silence for a while the only noise that was heard was that made by Sandra as she sobbed.

"Ok, what about the second shooting?" asked Jadanick.

"Do you have something to drink?" asked Emma.

"Sure," replied Sandra getting up to fetch soft drinks from the kitchen. She returned and gave Emma the orange juice.

"The second time, happened some years later when I was seventeen. I think the same people tracked me down where I was in-hiding. I was ambushed, I got shot and when I searched for someone to subjugate there by giving myself chances to survive your name appeared again on the radar. After that time, I knew that if I stayed there I was going to die, so I ran.

"So, who killed your parents and why? Are these people still following you? Are they going still to follow you here?" asked Jadanick.

"My parents were killed by the people my dad worked for. The last days before Christmas they had been to our home searching for missing money, so they said. My dad had showed them all his bank accounts and investments. I think there was some missing money and my dad was one of the suspects so they say. But I think there was some illegal dealings going on and my dad threatened to report them so they killed him,".

"So, how do I fit in all this in your world?"

asked Jadanick "Honestly, that's what I have been trying to find out myself. Apart from saving lives especially mine I do not know yet. I think you might be one of us," said Emma.

"What do you really mean when you say one of us?" asked Jadanick.

"I mean one of the seven Emperor's bodyguards," replied Emma. Jadanick looked at his girlfriend in astonishment.

"I knew there was some royalty about you, my Darling," said Sandra smiling at Jadanick.

"Thanks babe," replied Jadanick.

"Emperor bodyguards for real? So how do we meet this Emperor and where is he right now?" asked Jadanick.

"That is a good question. That is why I came here. We should have started at an early stage, normally at the age of seven. Normally per the legend initiation starts at the age of seven. For unknown reasons, we did not commence initiation for several reasons. On the eve of my seventh birthday I was about to leave my parents to initiate service but somehow, I received a message asking me to abort and wait for further instructions. The reason then was that the Emperor was not located or was not born yet. So, I fall in a trance for days and telepathically I communicated with Alina, one of us. I found out that they were having problems of finding the Emperor so none of us were synchronized. The Emperor when he is there we all get linked and synchronized automatically. Early this century when the world changed when the ozone layer was destroyed that is when the problems began. The priests lost touch with the Emperor. All the telepathy communication ended or were lost. At the age of seventeen I was in and out of the trances which is a sign of calling and on the eve of my eighteenth birthday a ship came for me from Russia and here I am. The Emperor I guess has been located," explained Emma.

"So, what about you any signs of your calling?" asked Emma. Jadanick kept quiet for a while, he looked at Sandra and put his hand around her.

"I must confess the day I got shot I had

received a message too to wait for a ship in the park on the eve of my birthday. So, on the 24th of December here I am in the park waiting for the ship with my friends. Then came these rival boys and before I knew it, I had a bullet wound and I was on the ground. All these years there were saying that the rival boys shot me but I knew something more sinister was behind this," said Jadanick.

"See, all the Emperor bodyguards were born on the same day and they all have birth marks or tattoos on their shoulders," said Emma.

"I do not have a birthmark or a tattoo," replied Jadanick.

"But you were born on 25th of December, right?" asked Emma.

"Yes. I was born on Christmas day," replied Jadanick.

"Alina too was born on Christmas day," added Emma.

"So, who crash-landed, you or Alina?" asked Jadanick

"I do not know about that, I landed safety in the lake outside the city. It could be any of the others," replied Emma.

"So, our task right now is to find the Emperor and start our service, protecting, and honoring him," added Emma.

"Only if we know how to find this Emperor," replied Jadanick.

"So how come you do not wear a watch and you said that you do not have a tattoo. I do not understand how you appeared on my radar?" asked Emma.

"Ok. Honestly, I was born with this tattoo," Jadanick removed his shirt and showed Emma the tattoo on his back shoulder.

"Waal your tattoo is very big as compared to mine," replied Emma.

"So, what is your tattoo about," asked Jadanick.

"Sign of the sun," replied Emma.

"What about yours?" asked Emma.

"Honestly, I do not know exactly, but it is some kind of ancient art. I have not looked at it properly," replied Jadanick. The bodyguard knocked and entered the lounge room and signaled something to Jadanick.

"Ok, we will start preparations," replied

Jadanick to the bodyguard.

"As you know we must fly to the world above otherwise, we will freeze to death here on earth," said Jadanick.

"Ok, thank you for everything, I better be going," replied Emma getting up to go.

"No. Stay with us for now. I will fly you there," replied Jadanick.

"Thank you," replied Emma. .

CHAPTER SIX

Weeks after, Emma was in the library when she suddenly started feeling unwell. Soon afterwards she collapsed and fainted. Help was called, and she was rushed to the first aid room in one of the rooms in the complex encompassing the library.

"Hello. Where is the library?" asked Alina. "A few minutes down the road in the complex you won't miss it. If lost just ask anyone in there," replied the gate office attendant. Alina walked down the road and she entered the complex. This was a modern built complex but some buildings inside looked as if they were just renovated. She reached the entrance of the building housing the library. She stood there for a while looking around. Suddenly a strange feeling struck. She felt like she has been there before. She heard a beeping sound and looked at her watch. A message was displayed on the screen.

'Synchronizing completed.'

Alina looked worried for a moment. Quickly she scrolled down her watch and searched for who she had been synchronized with.

"What! That can't be right!" she spoke to herself loudly.

"Unknown entity? I have not heard of that before. I thought you can only get synchronized with entities with genuine not hidden identities," explained Alina talking to herself. Quickly she switched off the watch and took out the small box that jams signals and placed the watch inside. She put the small box back into her bag.

She entered the library and looked around. She walked through the isle looking everywhere for any suspicious persons. She went to the e- books sections and somehow, she was about to sit on the chair when she stood up involuntarily and walked to the other section and sat down. As soon as she has sat down she had a flash image of Emma fainting.

"It's Emma," she spoke aloud. Quickly she got up and was about to go toward the door when she felt a feeling of fear. She went back into the library and hide in the isle looking at the library entrance. A man with blonde hair suddenly appeared on the door and looked at his watch. He waited at the door just like what Alina had done and afterwards entered the library. He did not look friendly. Alina ran toward the back of the library into the kitchen and through another door. She was about to go outside through the back door when she saw a man standing outside. Fear struck her. She thought that they might be two of them so she went back into the building. She found one door and approached the door. She opened the door and inside looked like a big document or study room. She looked around, and it seemed that the room hadn't been used for a very long time. She looked around and approached a door. She tried to open the door, but the door was looked. She looked around again and went out of this room back into the room she had passed through but this time went through a different door. This room was very cold than most of the rooms and it was not well lit. In the middle of the room was something like an altar. At first it looked like a church altar but the room was not that big. She was about to leave when the stones on the altar started glowing. These were the green stones. She walked slowly toward the glowing stones. She saw a marking on the altar and stopped. She had seen that marking before. She tried to think where she saw the marking but she could not. She thought that maybe it was from the library. Slowly the stones were releasing the smoke. The whole room turned into a beautiful fluorescent green color. She started walking around the room looking for anything that can give her clues. She came across a wall with picture frames. She stood there, looked at the pictures on the wall and she fell into a trance. The siren rung and everyone started evacuating earth going to the world above. Everyone left, and the library was closed. After eleven at night the gates were closed and earth was deserted. Just after eleven at night Alina woke up shivering with cold. She looked disoriented. Where am I? Was the first question that came to her mind. She looked around and remembered the green stones glowing on the altar. She got up and switched on the lights. The lights in there were dimmer than the rest. She tried to put everything together. She remembered falling into a trance after looking at the photos. She quickly took out the small box from her bag and took her watch out. She switched it on and wore it. She looked at the pictures again. There were seven pictures on the wall all with identical girls. To her surprise, she looked like them. Her watch beeped. She looked at the message and the message read that synchronizing failed. How come? She thought to herself. Fear struck again. Who is out there? It was when she checked the time of synchronizing failure that she discovered that the message referred to that time in the afternoon when she switched off her watch. She scrolled down and selected reboot and reset all parameters. The watch switched off and started rebooting. The room was getting colder and colder. She looked around and switched on the heaters. When the watch finished, rebooting Alina had lost all connections and links with anyone she had linked with before. She activated the search function, and the watched searched for anyone nearby with no luck. After some minutes a message appeared on the screen.

'Please find alternative power source. System shutdown in two hours. Subjugate or synchronize now.' Alina looked lost for ideas. Who should she synchronize with? Quickly she activated the search function, and the system started searching again. In the end the no entity found message was displayed on the watch's screen. She looked for anything to keep her warm. After one hour, the lights and power went off. It started getting cold. Alina as a last resort quickly touched her tattoo and waited. After sometime she touched her tattoo again and waited. After some minutes, she tried the search function on her watch.

"Come on anyone. Help. Where are you? I might die down here," said Alina speaking loud. This time temperatures had plummeted to minus degrees and ice was starting to develop.

'System shutdown in less than ten minutes,' message appeared on the screen. She scrolled again and tried to synchronize but with failure. She was really feeling cold. She sat down and touched her tattoo again and waited. Slowly she started dozing off. This time she didn't stop holding the tattoo. She looked at her watch again and tried for the final time before everything shuts down. She activated the search function again. She dozed off for a minute while the search was on. She was woken up by a beep sound and she looked at the message on the screen, that read, synchronizing successful. As soon as synchronizing was completed her system started charging. She reprogrammed her watch to subjugate and synchronize respectively after every two minutes. This was the only way she can survive the night. She touched her tattoo and all night her body released energy to wade off the cold. Half way through the night she scrolled down her watch to find out who she was linked to and who she had synchronized to and the message came as an unknown entity. Alina fell asleep for hours. It was early in the morning that she received a message on her watch. The message read.

'I saved you tonight but I will kill you tomorrow: unknown entity.' Emma woke up and walked to the mirror. She felt weak. Something must have gone wrong. She looked in the mirror before screaming. "Damn! What happened to my eyes? My eyes have changed color?" said Emma talking to herself. She looked closely and somehow, she saw Alina.

"Alina?" she spoke out aloud. She sat down for a while trying to make sense of all this.

This is the first time this has happened. Quickly she went into the bedroom and took her bag. She opened it and took a small box out. She opened the box and took out her watch before wearing it. She took a long breath out before switching the watch on. She activated the search mode, and a message appeared on the screen. 'Searching in progress please wait.'. She waited impatiently, the knock on her bedroom door sends her flying.

"Emma, are you okay its Sandra? Just checking if you are OK?" shouted Sandra from the other side of the door.

"I am okay I will be out in a minute or two," replied Emma. A no entity found message appeared on the screen. Emma went out to talk to Jadanick and Sandra.

"I am not one hundred percent sure but I think Alina has arrived as well. I tried to search for her but I can't find her. She might be in invisible mode," said Emma showing her eyes to Jadanick.

"So, what does that mean?" asked Jadanick. "It starting to make sense now. That day I was in hospital is the first day

Alina arrived. I fell in a trance in the Library near the gate. I presume she was there at that time or anywhere nearby. This allowed me and her to be synchronized and after that we will be linked together," said Emma.

"So, you mean that she can take bullets for you now instead of me?" asked Jadanick with a big grin on his face. They all laughed for a while.

"No, you still take bullets for me. I mean for everyone," said Emma cunningly.

"But why do I have to die for everyone," asked Jadanick not expecting a reply from Emma. Emma leaned forward and asked Jadanick to lean forward as well.

"Look. Do you mind if I call you Jay?" asked Emma putting her face in front of Jadanick.

"It's okay go ahead," replied Jadanick.

"See Jay. I have this watch. If something bad is about to happen to me. It takes me only two to three seconds to subjugate. What about you what would you do?" asked Emma.

"I do not know girl what do you expect me

to do?" replied Jadanick.

"Where you got that watch from. If I am a part of all this why I do not have a watch too?" asked Jadanick.

"Honestly I do not know. I got mine the day I was supposed to leave at the age of seven," replied Emma.

"Ah now I see. I remembered looking for the watch too that night I got shot. So, someone else might have found the watch," explained Jadanick.

"That explains the hostile unknown entity showing on my radar. Okay that's sorted out. We have to get the watch back," replied Emma.

"I know who can help us," said Jadanick. That afternoon they contacted someone Jadanick thought might help them.

"Natasha, please meet Emma. Emma meet Natasha." The women exchanged greetings over a coffee. They talked and Natasha agreed to take them to someone who can help them. They had just finished having their coffee when a blonde man appeared from nowhere. He entered the coffee shop and looked at his watch. He raised his arm as if to get a better signal. Slowly he moved in the coffee shop looking at everyone. Jadanick looked at Emma as if asking if it was the guy with his watch. He gave Emma a signal and Emma quickly touched her watched and scrolled down. As the man arrived at the table Jadanick was seated. Jadanick stood up and wrestled the man trying to remove the watch from the man's wrist. The fight broke out. Every time Jadanick hit the man his eyes glittered and changed color. The man seemed not to feel anything. It was not long before Jadanick was floored to the ground. Jadanick looked at Emma.

"Behind you!" all the woman shouted as the man approached to attack Jadanick from behind. The fight went on and Jadanick was on the ground again.

"You got me shot and you just watch when I am getting my ass kicked. Woman do something subjugate!" shouted Jadanick. Emma looked confused for a while.

"I do not know if that's possible if it's not me," said Emma looking at Natasha and Sandra. Quickly she scrolled down her watch and activated the search mode. "Come on! Come on!" she shouted looking at her watch. Unknown Entity identified message appeared on the screen. She chooses the lock and prepare to subjugate option. The please wait message appeared on the screen. This time Jadanick was received a thorough beating. She looked at the watch again. An unable to lock entity message appeared on the screen. She looked at Jadanick and shook her head. Sandra had called Jadanick's bodyguards through the device in her bag. The bodyguards entered the coffee shop and pointed the gun at the blonde man who instantly flipped a button on his watch. "No! No! Do not shot!" shouted Jadanick and Emma. The man stood there with a big grin on his face. Moments later he was on the floor. Sandra screamed and everyone looked around to see who fired the shot. Sandra knelt on the floor holding Jadanick in her arms. The door opened quickly and the other bodyguard entered looking surprised. He stood there for a few seconds before rushing to where Jadanick was.

"I swear I took that guy out only. I fired one shot. You got to believe me I did not shoot the boss," shouted the bodyguard. No one seemed to be concerned about him he just stood there looking at the other bodyguards trying to convince them that he did not shoot his boss, Jadanick. No one seemed to take notice of the blonde man. Everyone was looking at Jadanick. It was minutes later when Emma looked at her watch which was flashing. Synchronizing completed: unknown entity, a message appeared on her screen. Quickly she got up to take the watch off the blonde man but he was no longer there.

"Oh. No!" shouted Emma. They all stopped and looked at Emma.

"What's wrong?" asked Natasha.

"The man," said Emma pointing at the place the blonde man was lying.

"He is gone?" shouted the bodyguard who had shot him.

"Where did he go? I do not know what's going on but I swear I did not shoot the boss. I swear by my kids. Marius, you believe me, right? Mako. Right?" asked the bodyguard trying to gage the other bodyguard's views. It was Emma who comforted the bodyguard.

"I know you did not. I believe you. We all believe you. It's okay," Further away in the city a lady has just fell. She is clutching her shoulder. She is bleeding. She has been shot. People are rushing to the scene. A man knelt to see how he can help the woman.

"Call the ambulance quickly," shouted the man to another onlooker.

"You are going to be fine just hang in there. Ambulance is on its way." Soon afterwards the ambulance arrived and took the woman to the hospital.

"What happened?," asked the receiving nurses at the hospital.

"Not sure a possible gunshot victim. No identification. Vital signs okay," replied one of the ambulance crews. Quickly she was rushed to the operating room. Minutes later another ambulance arrived. A man is put on the trolley bed and rushed to the operating room in the room next door to the shot lady. The senior nurse quickly called for extra help.

"We have two victims with gunshot wounds doctor Vaal to operating room two and doctor Nilee to operating room one please." The medical staff rushed around doing what they do best. After an hour or so the two doctors left the operating rooms and are walking down the corridors.

"Vaal, how was your patient? Something strange about mine. She has been shot but somehow. I could not find the bullet or any bullet fragments. There is no bullet powder or anything. I think in my career this is the first time I have witnessed this," said doctor Nilee stopping and looking at doctor Vaal. Doctor Vaal was putting on his reading glasses.

"My patient his body is riddled with bullets wounds. I think he is lucky to be alive. I think he has been here before. You know these musicians they kill each other for nothing. I think he is lucky this time he has been shot on his shoulder. The bullet missed any vital organs, it's a through, through case," replied doctor Vaal.

"Does that mean you could not find the

bullet as well?" asked doctor Nilee.
"I couldn't find anything, true," replied doctor Vaal. Alina woke up with pain on her shoulder. She looked around and found out that she was in a hospital. She sat down on the hospital bed. She looked on her left hand but her watch was gone. She looked around and saw a key on the table. She looked around and saw a locker. She stood up and walked toward it. She opened the locker and took out her stuff. She opened the small box and took out her watch. She wore it and switched it on. She scrolled the last entry, and it was a confirmation that she was synchronized to Jadanick and that they were linked now. Quickly she took the hospital phone and called the operator.
"Hello. How can I help you?" asked the operator.
"I am looking for Jadanick. Can you find out if anyone in this hospital is by that name? Please will you," pleaded Alina.
"Hold the line I will put you through to someone who can help," replied the operator. Alina waited hoping to hear good

news.

"Hello. How can I be of any help?" asked the receptionist at the foyer.

"Hey. I am a relative and I would like to know if there is someone by the name of Jadanick in here," asked Alina.

"I will check for you hold the line," replied the receptionist.

"Sorry the only Jadanick was here a few months ago," replied the receptionist. Alina put the phone down and started pacing up and down in her hospital room. She walked toward the walls next to room one where she has been placed after the operation and she felt something like a flash of the time she was shot. She stood there for a while and went outside her room. She walked toward room one and waited outside, her heart beating very fast. She opened the door and came face to face with Jadanick. They both screamed at the same time and Jadanick slumped his head on the bed. Alina fell on the floor. The nurses came running and took Alina to her room.

"What happened?" asked one nurse talking

to the other.

"She might have been lost. Her room is just next to this one and probably just shocked to see someone else in her room," replied the other nurse. Emma and Natasha and Sandra arrived to see Jadanick that afternoon.

"There is a lady in this hospital. Just like you. You remember the first time we meet. Eh when we were both shot. Same. She is here. She opened my door and I..." Jadanick was speaking very fast talking to Emma.

"Slow down. It's okay. We will find her. Natasha come with me," said Emma about to leave the room with Natasha leaving Jadanick with Sandra. Before she left Emma collapsed on the floor. The two ladies rushed to her rescue.

"What's wrong Emma?" asked Sandra. Emma looked as if she was going to faint. As the two women were looking at her, her eyes changed color. She is normally a blue-eyed woman but her eyes changed to green.

"Put her on this bed," shouted Jadanick as

he got up from the bed.

"What is going on?" asked Jadanick. The two ladies did not say anything, they just looked at each other in shock. They had never witnessed something like this before. Emma fell into a trance. Suddenly the door opened a woman stood on the door. They all panicked thinking it was that blonde man.

"Who are you?" asked Jadanick. The woman did not reply, but she walked inside slowly and straight to the bed where Emma was sleeping. Jadanick, Sandra and Natasha all looked at each other in disbelief. She looked like Emma. She was identical to Emma. She had green eyes too. They all walked slowly toward her with their heads lowered down trying to see clearly.

"Are you twin sisters?" asked Sandra.

"So, it's not Emma. So, who then?" asked Alina with a soft voice as if asking just herself. She turned around and looked Jadanick in the eyes.

"It's you! Why? Who are you? Why are you trying to get me killed? Who are you?"

asked Alina pushing Jadanick away.

"Are you Alina?" asked Jadanick.

"Yes. I am Alina. Who are you? Who is he?" asked Alina looking at Sandra and Natasha.

"I am one of you girls," added Alina looking at Natasha and Sandra. Sandra and Natasha just looked at each other without saying anything. After a while when Alina restarted the conversation.

"When did you ladies arrive? Did you find the Emperor? How come you all do not have watches?" asked Alina sensing something wrong.

"What happened to Emma did she get shot?" asked Jadanick sacred for Emma.

"No. We are synchronizing and linking up. This is the first time we are together you know? What I do not understand is that why only her? You too you should have gone into a trance. Unless." Alina did not finish talking. She had realized that only Emma was one of them.

"Ok. I guess you are just Emma's friends," said Alina putting her hand in Emma's blouse and touching her on the back shoulder leaving her hand there for a while.

"We are just friends," replied Sandra.

"I guess so. What about you? You got shot too?" she asked Jadanick.

"I do not know really what happened. Eric tried to kill the man I was fighting with but someone I ended up being shot as well," added Jadanick.

"Ok. We have to wait for Emma to come around," added Alina. Later, Emma woke up. She was very excited to see Alina it felt like she had seen her sister. The two talked for a very long time before all decided to go with Natasha. They jumped into Jadanick's car and they left the hospital.

"We are here. Let me talk to this guy first. Ok? He might freak out," said Natasha getting out of the car. She closed the car door and waited outside a tall gate. The intercom system was switched on and Natasha spoke with the person on the other end. The camera on top of the gate pointed at Natasha and then at Jadanick's car. Natasha spoke again using the intercom system. Moments later the gate opened and everyone got out of the car. They entered through these tall gates. They waited for the door to open after a while a buzzer is heard and the door opened. They went straight down the basement. Teekay was a very short guy. He wore glasses and a cap.

"What brings you here this time Nat? In trouble, again?" asked Teekay sipping his vodka glass.

"Easy with that we need you fresh and sober," said Natasha.

"Me. With this or not I am still the same. What can I do for you Nat?" asked Teekay hold Natasha in her waist. This time I want you to help my friends here.

"We want to find a way of locating and getting a lock-on an entity," said Emma.

"What kind of entity?" asked Teekay.

"Special one probably one you have never encountered before," replied Alina.

"No job too big or too small for me. Ask Nat," said Teekay jokingly.

"Yeah right. Just get us what we want?" said Natasha blushing. Teekay sat down and started entering coordinates on the keyboard.

"Do you have last coordinates and the position in space?" asked Teekay. Emma quickly scrolled down her watch and showed it to Teekay. The typing went on for some time before Teekay cursed.

"Damn! I cannot triangulate him but I am very close. He is a kind of jamming my signal. Ok wait watch this," said Teekay flipping one button.

"With this single button, I have gone into invisible mode. Now I am not just searching, I am tracking as well ready to get a lock-on. Come on babe!" shouted Teekay looking at the screen. After a while Teekay cursed again.

"This guy changes position and coordinates every 2 minutes I can't put a lock-on him. He is a kind of shifting and acting as someone else's every time," said Teekay lifting his glass.

"I think I know what he is doing. He is subjugating every 5 minutes. No wonder why Jadanick couldn't knock him down," said Emma.

"See. I told you I could have kicked his ass

all over the coffee room. I knew it. He was cheating," said Jadanick feeling relieved to hear that after being butt-kicked in the coffee shop.

"Can we try to jam his signals and put a lock-on him," asked Jadanick.

"I have an idea I think the best is to match him too," said Teekay.

"What do you mean?" asked Natasha.

"We do whatever he does for the mean time and when we have a lock- on him, then we can jam his signals and subjugate him. If we can do that that will be his end," said Teekay.

"One question any chance we can block him so that he cannot subjugate or it will be great if we can re-subjugate back to him instantly?" asked Alina.

"These are all possibilities but his system is closed. Unless...," said Teekay hugging Natasha.

"You two you have a thing going on? Ya?" asked Sandra before everyone broke into laughter for a while.

"What you can do next time if you see him. Quickly activate synchronization mode and quickly let me know giving me your coordinates. I will be able to map and retrace his path once I have a pattern of his activities I will be able to deduce coordinates that matches his. Once that's done we will be able to put a lock-on him," said Teekay.

"Ok. We better be going guys," said Emma.

"Nat babe come and see me, sometime will you?" asked Teekay kissing Natasha.

"Ok. Teekay? When all this is over, I will come, and see you. Ok?" said Natasha. Everyone left, jumped into the car and the car drove off.

"Where is the Emperor guys?" asked Emma.

"Hard to tell. I think the question should be where are the others? We should be seven. Where are the rest?" asked Alina.

"Assuming I am one of you where are the other four? Did you crash land when you arrived here? Did someone beat the hell out of you?" asked Jadanick looking at Alina.

"Me. No. I arrived safely landed in a lake outside the city. I got shot only," replied

Alina.

"So, there is someone who crash-landed. And someone got beaten up very badly," said Jadanick.

"We should try to find the others first," said Emma.

"How? Any ideas? I think everyone is in invisible mode. We will keep on trying," replied Alina.

"I think I know where the earlier Emperor was. I came across this place. For some time, I was shocked that much that I fell in a trance. The next time I woke up I was stuck alone here on earth. I spent one night here on earth," said Emma.

"Me, too once," replied Alina. Everyone looked at each other. That can't be true. "How did you survive the night?" asked Jadanick.

"Hooked up to an unknown entity and subjugated every two minutes," said Emma.

"Ah now I see. You rather get me killed, ya? He served you and I am the price. So, you let me get shot," quipped Jadanick. The other laughed they knew Jadanick was just joking.

"Ok guys on a serious note, I know where the former Emperor lived. Near the gate. In fact, the gate, that tower was part of the old Emperor's tower. There are buildings in the new complex and the underground ones belonged to the Emperor," said Emma.

"Now I see why I feel strange whenever I am there," added Alina.

"I think we should go there straight away and find out," added Jadanick. The car was driven toward the gate in the city. Silence broke out in the car everyone was just imaging what the future holds for them

CHAPTER SEVEN

Weeks after the ladies and Jadanick came face to face with the man with the blonde hair. Quickly Emma contacted Teekay. She gave him her coordinates.

"Give me back my watch or else you die," shouted Jadanick confronting that blonde man. He just smiled and quickly scrolled down his watch.

"This time I won't leave you alive. I fight to kill," said the blonde man fast and loud. The fight broke out. They fought for some time before the blonde man was floored to the ground. Quickly he scrolled down his watch, and the fight resumed.

"Quickly Teekay. Did you manage to?" asked Emma.

"Not yet keep him busy. I want to jam his signals so that first he can't use any of you as the subjugate entity after that then bounce back to him so that in the end he is the one who will pay. See what I mean?" shouted Teekay from the other end of the phone line.

"Ok. Hurry," replied Emma. They fought for some time. All this time it was only Jadanick reacting to the punches and the kicks. The blonde man all the time remained solid apart from the first time he saw floored by Jadanick. He kept scrolling down his watch. After sometime Jadanick would punch him but he would not react very much, then comes a time when suddenly, he reacted like he had been given the heaviest blow. He slumped on the ground and for the first time started bleeding. He got up and in shock and touched his lips and wiped blood. He tried to advance before he acted like he had been punched in the head and he fell back to the ground. Jadanick remembered the day something like that happened to him when he was in the hospital. He started jumping up and down twist crossing his legs. The blonde man stopped and looked at his watch. He scrolled down his watch and screamed.

"Damn! What is happening?" Jadanick this was his chance, so he started advancing. He punched the blonde man, but he did not react straight away. Even him he just stood there surprised. Then seconds later he fell to the ground holding his mouth. More blood was coming out from his mouth. Emma signaled the OK sign. Jadanick pulled his gun and aimed at the blonde man who in a fraction of a second subjugated. He stood there looking at Jadanick with a big grin on his face.

"You are going to commit suicide," said the blonde man looking at Jadanick. Confused and scared Jadanick looked at the ladies, first at Emma, then Alina, then Natasha and lastly at his girlfriend Sandra.

"Kill him Darling he tried to kill you," shouted Sandra. Jadanick did not hesitate to pull the trigger. It all happened in slow motion. The blonde man saw every move of the bullet coming to him. He did not even move, he smiled and took the bullet and fell to the ground. Sandra just as a reflex ran to hug Jadanick fearing the worst. A few seconds later he fell to the ground. Alina was about to ran to Jadanick's rescue when she fell too. Then the worst happened when Emma fell too. It all happened in a few seconds. The blonde man got up and sat on the ground looking at everyone. Jadanick got up too and touched himself. He had no gun wound just the impact like pain. He looked at his hands, he had no blood. He tried to get up but Sandra hold him down. Alina got up too and sat on the ground touching herself. She had the just impact pain. "Emma!" she screamed and quickly got up and ran to where Emma was. She picked her up putting her head on her legs. Emma opened her eyes and checked herself for any injuries.

"Did I get shot?" asked Emma fearing for the worse.

"I think you are okay I do not feel or see

any blood," replied Alina. So, everyone was okay so what happened. Nick was asking himself. All this time the blonde man was busy playing with his watch and soon after he was heard laughing cunningly after looking at his watch. Everyone looked at each other and they all took cover. He looked at his watch again and laughed even worse. He walked away and left. Nobody said anything they all stayed on the ground taking cover. Minutes later there was still silence and everyone was still on the ground.

"Jay, are you okay?" shouted Emma.

"I am okay. You?" asked Jadanick.

"We are all fine," replied Alina. They all got up.

"What happened?" asked Emma confused about all this.

"Honestly I do not know but it seemed the bullets has been bouncing from one place to another. Who got it last I do not know," shouted Jadanick. There were in the middle of the conversation when Teekay phoned them.

"Are you all okay? I got the Douchebag.

Did you see what I did. I jammed his signal. So, whatever he did bounced back to him. He looks dead to me he has not moved a bit on the radar," explained Teekay excited about all this.

"But he walked away. I saw him walk away," said Emma in shock.

"What did Teekay say?" asked Jadanick.

"He said he is dead. On the radar, he is not moving?" replied Emma.

"Dead? Is he crazy? Dead my ass. I saw the dude wriggling his… butt… going that way with a big smile on his face. So, how come he is saying that he is dead?" asked Jadanick.

"I do not know that's what he said," replied Emma.

"Probably he is showing on his radar that time he was lying on the ground. His reading on the radar could be delayed with some minutes," replied Alina. That was the only perfect explanation, they got in the car and drove off. Shane had waited for this journey for the past eleven years. He was born in Antarctica. He had refused going to school, seeing no point as he was going to be the Emperor's bodyguard. After the age of seven he had waited for this journey. At the age of seven on eve of his birthday he had received a message in a trance to go and board the ship but somehow the ship didn't arrive. He found the watch though. Ever since he knew he was destined for great things. He expected the calling to be soon after the age of seven. It has been eleven years now but hopes are still the same. Protecting and preserving the Emperors bloodline was his eternal duty. Nothing was going to stop him from doing that. On Christmas eve, the ship did not turn up. This time he started doubting the whole thing. What he couldn't understand was why he did not start at the age of seven as in the legend. Christmas, he spent thinking about this journey. It was after Christmas that one day he just fell asleep and slept the whole day. He went into a trance where he received the message. He was now required to start serving the Emperor. A ship this time came, and he left for the United States of America where the Emperor had lived the last century. This was the only safe country for the Emperor until mid-century. He sat off in his spaceship. The spaceship arrived safely in the lake outside the city. He got off the spaceship and was about to go to the city when he heard a beeping sound coming from his watch. He looked and saw the wait searching in progress message. He was very excited, quickly he started going to the city leaving the spaceship in the lake. He had just walked a few meters when his watch started flashing. He looked at it. A message was on the screen asking him to accept or deny a synchronizing request. This is the first time he had seen the message, so he accepted synchronizing. Another beep sound went off, and he looked at his watch again. It was confirmation that synchronizing was completed, and he was linked to an unknown entity. He stopped and looked at the watch's screen.

"Unknown entity?!" he shouted to himself and stopped. Quickly he turned back and started walking back toward the spaceship. He quickly tried to scroll down and remove the link but somehow, he was now locked-on to this unknown entity. He panicked and opted to remove any links and activate the invisible mode. It took more time than it should normally do. He quickly removed the watch and walked fast back to the ship. He was about to enter the ship to reset the watch when the watch let out a beep sound. He looked at the watch and there was a message on the flashing screen. Danger of death subjugate now or activate invisible mode... Ten seconds remaining. The countdown began, 9 seconds, 8 seconds... 7 seconds. Shane panicked quickly he tried to subjugate but subjugating unknown entity was unsuccessful. It took two more seconds to search for another entity. He realized that his best option was to hide in the ship. He quickly rushed to the spaceship but a few meters from the spaceship he felt a sharp pain and he dropped the watch in the lake. He fell in the lake too. Weeks later Emma came running to Jadanick and Alina and the other girls.

"I have located someone else at the gate I

think he is one of us," said Emma breathing heavily.

"This is the second time now. The first time I thought he could be hostile but I think he is one of us. He switches on his visible mode at the gate then after that he switches to invisible," added Emma.

"What makes you think that he is friendly?" asked Jadanick.

"Instincts I guess. Whoever that person is switch off visibility mode whenever he leaves the gate. Just like we do. All the unknown entities do not hide but you can just link to them," added Emma.

"Maybe she is right. Do you want to go and check it out?" asked Alina. They all agreed and Jadanick drove to the city gate. They arrived and waited. It was Emma who suggested spending sometime in the library researching about the Emperor while waiting for this person. There was nothing regarding the recent Emperor. There were few stories of the previous Emperor who had the magnificent warriors but no one knew what happened to them. Emma took this opportunity to show everyone the place she had discovered before. They all entered the place. It was like an Emperor's palace for sure. In its glory days, the palace would have qualified as the residence of the Emperor or someone very rich. It was well built. There were big rooms inside well decorated. Emma led them to the room with the magic stones. She advised everyone not to stay in there for too long just to check the pictures on the wall. They all could not believe what they were seeing.

"Surely the photos look like the two of you. The resemblance is striking. There must be an explanation to this," quipped Jadanick.

"Let's take the pictures. We take only the two that match you and Alina," said Jadanick. "Ok gate the pictures do not stay too much in that room," warned Emma. They all left the room with the magic stones and entered the other rooms. They looked for anything that can give them hints but there was none. They went into the other room that looked like the lounge area. It had a cabinet. They went there and tried to open it. It seemed that the cabinet was locked. They looked for the key but did not find the key. Jadanick tried to break the door cabinet, but he failed. Emma went to the other room that looked like it was used as the kitchen. She opened the drawers and took out a knife before returning to the cabinet. She struggled with the door. The others left her in there and proceeded to the other rooms. The bell started to ring.

"What's that for?" asked Natasha.

"Let's go everyone. Hurry. There are about to close the complex you do not want to be locked in here," shouted Emma hysterical. They all started going back through the library and outside the complex.

"Alina quickly looked at her watch and searched for anyone. The search retained nothing, and they kept searching. They stayed there for some time before they decided to go. Jack arrived at the gate like always and turned his visibility mode to active. He waited for a while looking for anyone but everyone seemed more concerned about escaping the cold earth than with anything else. He waited there for a while not hoping to find anyone. That is when his watch started flashing. Unknown entity was in the vicinity. He quickly hid among the people. The blonde man arrived. He stood there for some time looking at his watch. The watched beeped and the blonde man looked at Jack. Jack pretended like he was someone not important. Slowly the man started walking toward Jack looking at his watch. He arrived at Jack and looked at him for some time.

"Are you one of us?" asked the blonde man.

"I do not know what you are talking about," replied Jack. The blonde man showed Jack his watch.

"Are you one of us? How come I feel strange around you?" asked Jack looking at the man.

"We have not synchronized each other yet and we are still not linked," replied the blonde man.

"Come with me I will take you to the

Emperor," said the man. Jack on hearing this he followed the man. They walked for some time toward the complex housing the library. It felt real, but he had one concern though. The weather.

"How the Emperor manage to survive this cold weather," asked Jack. The blonde man seemed not know what to say.

"Emperor has warriors that provides all that," replied the blonde man. That was true that's why there were there.

"So, where are the others?" asked Jack.

"Some came a few years ago, but for some reason they runaway possibly scared of the weather so the Emperor needs you," replied the man. The man tried to open the door to one of the buildings but the door was locked. He moved to the next one, and the door was locked too. That put Jack off and he stood there. The man tried the next door, and the door was not locked. He opened the door and waited for Jack. Jack stood there for some time thinking if this was a good idea or not. He walked toward the man carefully. He let the blonde man enter first into the building and he followed him. The building looked like no one has been in there for years.

"Give me your watch now or you die," asked the blonde man.

"Show me the Emperor first," replied Jack. The fight broke out.

"I do not want to kill you. Show me where the emperor is then I will let you go," said Jack. The blonde man kept fighting trying to take the watch from Jack. Jack stopped and looked at the blonde man. He walked toward the door and closed the door from the inside. He stopped a few feet from the door. He scrolled down his watch and removed his shirt. He touched his tattoo, and he fell to the ground and soon after a loud growling is heard and the blonde man was heard screaming. Two minutes later the sound died down. When Jack woke up, it was after eleven at night. The gate and been closed already. He woke up and saw the blonde man mauled to death. He knelt and removed the watch. He reset the watch and put it in his pocket. His only chance was to go to the spaceship. He left and headed to the ship. Emma had found

Chang's diary among the documents which were locked into the cabinet. She had hidden the diary from the rest of the group. She started reading it daily. It was later after reading Chang's diary that Emma revealed that she took a diary from the earlier Emperors' palace. The diary did shade some light on several issues.

"So, what did you find out about all this," asked Alina.

"It seems that somehow there were seven girls all with powers to protect the Emperor. They were associated with strange behavior. They all had tattoos which they used as powers somehow to protect the Emperor. They all started protecting the Emperor when they were seven years old," said Emma.

"So, what happened to them? Should there be information about them maybe their graves somewhere around here? That's what I was expecting," added Alina.

"I think we should all go there and buy that place and start leaving there, waiting for the Emperor," said Jadanick.

"I agree I think somehow we are meant to

live there. I felt connected to that place that night I slept there. It was cold, but it didn't feel as bad as I had expected. We should go back there again." A few weeks later they were back there. They took everything they possible needed and decided to spend the whole day there. With the help of the diary they let Alina sleep in the room with the magic stones. The time she entered there it seemed the sun was elevated. It became very hot inside. They looked at her tattoo and understood the role she had to play. They let Emma sleep in the room with the magic stones. All radio signals were jammed. So, her role was to help hide the Emperor's activities, so the enemy does not detect them. When Jadanick entered the room, nothing happened, so they knew he had no special role to play. Mid-century the world change and there were new threats to the survival of the Emperors. Threat no longer came from man alone, nature had become the Emperor's greatest enemy too. Sudden temperature fluctuations had meant sudden death to those loyal to the

Emperor. With no proper facilities to commute daily to the world above surely, they had to find another way. A new form of protection was needed. A new form of warriors was needed. New weapons were now needed. It was like back to the early years. The weather had changed. Earth was no longer habitable at night. The sudden temperature changes meant instant death. Meanwhile the biggest question was the whereabouts of the Emperor. They had searched everywhere with no luck. Jadanick came across a room that they used to store goods and other items. This room was in the basement. "Guys come and see this," shouted Jadanick. They all came downstairs. "What are these big drums and look at all this?". Asked Sandra. There were the biggest drums they had ever seen. They were from floor to the ceiling and big. There were about seven of them in that big room. At first, they thought they were for storing food. They had no openings. They concluded that somehow, they were for storing energy. They started looking at the other items. It seemed the items were removed from parts of the palace and brought here for safe keeping.

"Could it be a possibility that the Emperor had to go somewhere or possibly abandon this palace that all these items were brought here for safe keeping?" asked Natasha.

"Highly likely unless if they were moved after," replied Sandra.

"It looks like they were preparing for the bad weather. This room looks like the energy room. I think these were to store solar energy that could explain why they have gone all the way to the roof. The biggest threat now to the Emperor was no longer man. But the weather," said Jadanick looking at the big drums again.

"Let's say they knew the weather was going to be this bad. So, these were the solutions. They have laid the road for us. Can we try to find a way of making this work?" added Jadanick.

"You could be right. In Chang's diary, each girl had a role to play. There were seven of them all with different protection forms and roles. The drums are seven possibly each representing each magnificent warrior or it's just coincidental?" asked Emma.

"I think somehow I have a role to play about these drums. The tattoo I have is of the sun," explained Alina.

"In that diary, did you find out how it worked in the past?" asked Jadanick

"There has been mention of the magic stones. Not really sure if that refers to the green stones on the altar- like place in the room with the pictures," said Emma.

"I have an idea why not two people stay in here and Jadanick Alina and the rest go back to that room and see what happens," suggested Emma. Emma stayed in the room with the drums with Natasha and the rest went to the room with the magic stones. As they entered the room, the stones started releasing the smoke and glowing at the same time giving the room a green color. It didn't take long before Alina fell into a deep sleep. Sandra ran back to Emma and Natasha telling them that Alina was in a trance. Nothing had happened on the other side. Alina's watch beeped while she was in a trance. It started to flash and Jadanick saw a message on the screen the message read; subjugating entity identified press confirm to initiate or cancel. Jadanick pressed confirm, and the process started. After a few seconds a confirmation message was on the screen showing that subjugating was successful. A few minutes later Alina woke up. Sandra came back running to tell Jadanick and Alina that the drums were glowing and making the buzz sound.

"Is Emma okay? I ask you, Darling. Is Emma okay?" shouted Jadanick.

"Yes. She is okay. Why you ask? What did you do?" asked Sandra after sensing some tenseness in her boyfriend's voice.

"I do not know, I subjugated another entity but I do not know who? Let's go to Emma now," explained Jadanick. Jadanick explained to Emma what had happened and Alina scrolled on her watch and everyone looked to see who the entity was. "Adonis! Who is Adonis?" they all shouted at the same time.

"The big drums work now, they are for storing solar energy," shouted Natasha.

"So, the new climate meant new functions among the magnificent warriors," explained Emma.

"Ok. If Alina is to manage the energy reserve what is your role. I think we are overlooking something here?" asked Jadanick.

"I jam signals, in other words I hide the Emperor from being detected," explained Emma.

"That's what I am afraid of. The question which we should be asking ourselves is hiding from who?" said Jadanick.

Everyone looked worried from a moment.

"Hiding from enemies like that man who kicked your ass all over the coffee shop," replied Emma trying to ease the tension. They all started laughing even Jadanick saw the funny side of this.

"But on a serious note that dude was just a petty thief. I know he nearly killed me but I do not think this is what this is meant for. There could be real," Jadanick did not finish his sentence. Emma interrupted him.

"Look Jay, no need to scare people right now. I think it's nothing to worry about right now," said Emma.

"We are putting our lives at risk so, we have to know all the facts," added Jadanick

"I know you are worried about me Darling, but it's okay we are in this together," said Sandra.

"You have no protection whatsoever, if anything happens to you I do not think I will be able to forgive myself. These two they can protect themselves they have the watch you do not. If there is something dangerous out there, I must know," explained Jadanick.

"I promise I won't let anything happen to you Sandra or even you Natasha," said Emma, looking at both the women. They went to what appeared as the lounge area and all sat down having food.

"We all need to agree if we all can stay here tonight. We know how to fill those drums. I think by the time the sunset we will have stored enough energy to last us until tomorrow," said Emma, pausing, and looking at everyone. Sandra put her arms around Jadanick and her head on his chest. We all agree? Yes?" asked Emma. "Yes," they all replied. For the first time the whole group did not go to the new world above they risked being frozen to death and stayed on earth. Emma slept in the room with the magic stones and the rest slept in the next room.

CHAPTER EIGHT

Jack since he arrived he had slept in the spaceship just a few times. The spaceship's energy reserves had gone down to critical levels. Visiting the Lake was the ritual he had done since he arrived here and tonight was no different. He had been inside the spaceship. He was about to leave the spaceship for the night when suddenly a message appeared on the ship's screen. 'Solar recharging in progress', a message was displayed on the screen. This was only possible if one of the magnificent seven had activated the system remotely. He was very happy not only can he drive the spaceship once fully charged he can meet the other members as well. So, the search was on. For the first time, he deactivated the invisible mode and opted for the visible mode. After spending sometime in the spaceship, he made his journey back to the city to search for others. He arrived at the gate and looked at both the watches there was no signal at all. There was something strange about the whole place. He decided to enter the building where the blonde man had taken him to. He entered the buildings looking for any clues. It was getting darker and colder by the night. He activated heat seekers, and the sensors took him outside all these buildings and into the complex further down the road. He broke-in and entered the building. This building was generating enough heat to be habitable. He remembered reading it somewhere that this was the earlier Emperor's palace. As soon as he had entered the building both the watches started flashing. They both had messages on them.

"Entity for synchronizing identified to

synchronize now press enter or abort," message appeared on the screen. He quickly synchronized on his watch. He aborted on the other watch. It took some minutes before synchronizing was completed. He waited for some time while the watch was linking him to the other entity. After a while he started walking in the building searching for the others. He took the path followed by Emma and ended up in the room with the magic stones. He stood there and watched Emma sleeping. He slept next to her. Jadanick had a dream that night. This is the first time he had been in a trance since the days he was a kid. In his dream, he dreamt of the eve of his seventh birthday.

"Mummy it's my birthday tomorrow I am going to the city with my friend," shouted Jadanick leaving the family house. He ran outside and met his friend who was standing outside. The two boys ran toward the city.

"I am very happy today. I am going to start another life as a bodyguard of the Emperor somewhere far away," said Jadanick to his friend showing much happiness and enthusiasm.

"Far away leaving me? Can I go with you?" asked Noel.

"No, you cannot you have to be chosen," answered Jadanick.

"Chosen by who? Ask them to choose me too," requested Noel.

"It's being chosen when you are still in your mother's belly. After that you just knew it," replied Jadanick.

"So how are you going to get there?" asked Noel Jadanick stopped and with his eyes wide open replied Noel.

"Spaceship. By a spaceship. The spaceship is coming for me," replied Jadanick with great enthusiasm and anticipation.

"But first I have to go and get the watch. They said that the watch drives the spaceship. So now we are going to get the watch," added Jadanick.

"Who are they?" asked Noel. "The old man with the white hair and white beard in my dream," replied Jadanick. The boys walked for a while and came to a park. It had snowed, and it looked lighter outside because of the snow. They were about to go to the place where the watch was when the other boys arrived.

"Where do you think, you are going?" asked the leader of the rival group.

"Who wants to know? Mind your business," replied Noel.

"I will make it my business. This is our side we do not want to see you this side again okay?" added the leader of the rival group.

"Let's, just get the watch and go," said Jadanick .

"What if they steal the watch from us?" asked Noel scared of losing the watch. Noel wanted to go as well with Jadanick. Moments later Jadanick let out a scream and fell to the ground.

"Oh, that really hurts. What happened to me," asked Jadanick.

"Oh. You were shot. They shot you. Help! Help! Call the ambulance," shouted Noel. Jadanick was shot presumably by the rival group.

"Tell me where the watch is Jadanick. I will bring it to you," asked Noel. Jadanick had lost a lot of blood and he was feeling weak. He pointed to the fountain in the park before the ambulance crew took him and drove him to the hospital. He woke up in the hospital asking for his watch.

"My watch! Where is my watch? Did you get my watch? Did you find my watch?" Jadanick asked Noel.

"Darling what is wrong? You are having a bad dream wake up?", Sandra shook Jadanick waking him up. Jadanick woke up and sat down. He got up and entered the room with the magic stone.

"Who are you? Wake up," Jadanick asked Jack who was fast asleep. Emma woke up, so as Jack. As soon as Jack saw Jadanick he put his hand in his pocket.

"No! I would not do that if I were you. Take the hand out of your pocket slowly," shouted Jadanick.

"I am one of you, my name is Jack," said Jack looking at everyone. Alina, Natasha and Sandra heard the commotion, and all came running.

"It's okay," said Emma looking at Jadanick. Jack put his hand in his pocket and took out the watch.

"I guess this belongs to you," said Jack giving Jadanick the watch.

"Strange. I was dreaming about this…," Jadanick did not finish his sentence he took the watch and wore it. As soon as he had worn the watch he let out a growl of pain. He touched his tattoo and fell to the ground.

"It's all right. Synchronizing in progress," said Jack looking at Sandra who seemed worried more than everyone else. By the time Jadanick woke up everyone was gathered around Jack. They had been talking for an hour or more. Jack was the leader they were looking for. He was very knowledgeable and not afraid. He had managed to kill the blonde man. Even Jadanick knew he was one of them. The hunt for the Emperor had begun. The coming weeks saw them taking turns to wait at the gates in the city in search of the Emperor and the others. One sunny afternoon they were in the Emperor's palace when Jadanick looked at Sandra. He acted as if he was singing. Sandra understood what that meant quickly with

the help of the others they asked Jadanick to lie on the couch and they all hold him down. Nothing happened though apart from the fact that he fell into a trance. Soon afterwards Adonis entered the building. They straight away knew he was one of them. He talked about his crash-landing and how he was beaten up after breaking into an empty property the days he arrived. Jadanick woke up, and they talked for a very long time with Adonis. "I remembered the day I crash-landed. For some reason, I fell in a trance. Auto pilot was on. When I woke up I was way past the landing lake. I was supposed to land in that lake but somehow, I ended up crashing in the mountains above the lake. I had ten seconds before impact and unexpectedly I saw the subjugate now option. Man, you do not know how I felt that day. I had seconds to decide. I just subjugated and here I am today. If it wasn't for you, I could be dead now," said Adonis holding Jadanick's shoulder.
"You nearly killed me Man. You know. I spent days in hospital you know. To make

things worse, the day I was supposed to be released from the hospital then I had a thorough beaten," explained Jadanick.

"Bad luck man. That day I went looking for help. I came across this empty house. It had food and everything. So, I went inside and made myself at home. I thought it was abandoned. I fell asleep heaters full blast. I woke up being dragged outside not just by one but by five guys. They said I used the only resources they had. I had a proper beaten. If I didn't play dead, I could have been killed," said Adonis.

"Then a few weeks ago, I went back to my spaceship to assess the damage, and I received a call for help for a one Shane. The message just appeared on the screen and the power of the spaceship just died," added Adonis.

"A Shane? I do not know anyone by that name," replied Jadanick.

"I am sure it was a call from a one Shane. We can still check from my spaceship sometime if you have time. Ok?" asked Adonis.

"Ok," replied Jadanick.

"Ladies does anyone know anyone by the name of Shane?" asked Jadanick.

"Sounds familiar but I am not sure. Eh what happened?" asked Emma.

"He should be one of us. He appeared on Adonis radar asking for help a few weeks ago," replied Jadanick.

"Maybe we should go and see Teekay tomorrow he might be able to find him using his system," replied Natasha.

"Ok. We will see tomorrow if we have time," replied Adonis.

"So, what kind of tattoo do you have?" asked Adonis.

"Looks like some ancient language, no one seemed to know what it is. Above all it's not clear than it used to be. Bullets have tattooed my body too," said Jadanick showing Adonis his tattoo.

"So, you have been through a lot you. Ya?" asked Adonis.

"I think I received more than my fair share of bad luck the only good thing about all this is that it's all behind us. Seems the future is brighter," quipped Jadanick.

"What about you what kind of tattoo do

you have?" asked Jadanick. Adonis did not reply instead he removed his t- shirt and showed Jadanick.

"Damn! What language is that? Where are you from again?" asked Jadanick.

"I am from France, I speak French and trust me that is not French," replied Adonis.

"Girls we need your help come and see this," shouted Jadanick. The ladies came and surrounded Adonis trying to read his tattoo.

"What language is that?" asked Alina.

"Who knows we must try to find out maybe that's a clue of where to find the Emperor," said Emma.

"Let's see yours Jay?" asked Emma. Jadanick did not hesitate. Quickly he removed his shirt. They all gathered around him. His tattoo was the biggest with so match details that it was not easy to tell what it is. Some areas had been scared as he had bullet wounds.

"First, we must try to find out what language that is in then try to get some clues," said Alina.

"The library is just around the corner tomorrow we can go and find out," replied Emma.

"I am not one hundred percent sure but the symbols looks like languages in the arctic circles. I am from Austria I can recognize maybe just one or two alphabetical letters," said Jack.

"What about you Jack? What kind of tattoo do you have?" asked Emma. Jack waited for some time before he took off his shirt.

"A lion!" Shouted everyone. Jack was the king of the beasts. Jadanick knew why it was easy for Jack to overpower the blonde man.

"So, it means there are still dangers lurking everywhere otherwise why would we need a lion?" asked Natasha. No one replied they all looked at each other. Jadanick quickly hugged Sandra.

"I think we all will be fine. Nothing to worry about," replied Jack. Everyone went to bed. Natasha couldn't sleep, so she woke up and walked just checking the other rooms. She remembered the last time she was in the room with the big drums that that room was very warm. She felt a bit cold. Quickly she walked toward the room with the drums. She opened the door and entered quickly. She stopped and froze with fear. She slowly walked backwards and closed the door behind her before she ran back to where the others were. She slept without saying anything. In the morning, she was talking to Sandra.

"I still can't believe what I saw last night," said Natasha in a low voice.

"Where Natasha and what did you see," asked Sandra not really paying attention.

"I woke up last night and..," said Natasha before being interrupted by Jadanick.

"Darling. We will all be going to the library but if you want to stay you can stay here with Natasha."

"I am not staying here alone. I am going with everyone," said Natasha with a high voice showing some signs of fear.

"Are you sure you are okay?" asked Sandra.

"Yes. I am Okay," replied Natasha.

"So, you were saying?" inferred Sandra.

"Last night I woke up after midnight. I could not sleep so I took a walk and ended up in the room with the solar drums. I was feeling cold. So, I opened the door and entered the room," said Natasha pausing for a while. She breathed heavily before continuing.

"There were six animals each sleeping against each drum. I saw two lions, a brown one and a white one, a leopard and the other I did not see clearly what kind of animals they were. I nearly peed my pants with fear. I walked very slowly and closed the door behind me I went straight back to sleep," she finished talking and looked at Sandra. Sandra did not say anything she stopped what she was doing and looked at Natasha for a very long time.

"You do not believe me?" asked Natasha.

"I do not know what you are trying to do but it's not funny," said Sandra walking away from Natasha.

"Darling are you ready. We are all going to the library. Do you want to come?"

"I was thinking of taking a nap but I might as well come with you," said Sandra going with Jadanick. The whole group went to the library. They had written down the letters on Adonis tattoo. They searched in the library the meaning of the tattoo. To meet the Emperor, to serve, to protect and to honor him means to defeat evil first.

"This is the best translation as the language is in the Antarctica language. Does anyone here come from Antarctica?" asked Emma.

"Okay everyone the best translation I have so far is that one on my computer screen. The tattoo means that for us to meet the Emperor first we must defeat evil. What evil? Honestly, I do not know," said Emma. Natasha looked at Sandra with the kind of look that says I told you already.

"That sounds scarier I think. It was much better if it was written that first you must defeat your enemy? Evil. Can mean anything," explained Jadanick.

"How do we defeat evil?" asked Adonis.

"I think it's simple, by protecting the Emperor. Evil can be bad weather or our enemies," replied Alina.

"What about Jadanick's tattoo? Any luck

with the translation?" asked Emma.

"No luck at all. I am starting to think that Jadanick's is more of a map than any saying," said Jack.

"Ok listen up we have to go and see Teekay today and try to locate our missing friend Shane." That afternoon they left the library and headed toward the other side of the city. Teekay was home, and he was delighted to see Natasha.

"Hey Natasha, thanks for coming I have been thinking about you. I had a bad dream about you last night. I am glad you are okay," said Teekay embracing Natasha.

"I am okay Teekay. You thought I never visit. Ha? Look here I am," replied Natasha.

"What can I do for you. You have a new enemy or what?" asked Teekay looking surprised.

"No. No. We need help with finding our friend," said Emma.

"My pleasure that is the only thing I do best," replied Teekay and when Natasha looked at him he added.

"And drinking the vodka of course," After

he had switched his system-on Teekay
asked for coordinates. Adonis scrolled his
watch and gave Teekay the coordinates.
Teekay typed in a lot of figures on his
keyboard.

"Bingo!" shouted Teekay.

"Can you also let us know where we can
find that person," asked Emma.

"No problem," replied Teekay After a
while he brings up a map showing the
actual place on the map.

"He is in a kind of lake. Wait, a minute,"
said Teekay zooming on the screen.

"He is in a lake, just outside the city," said
Teekay.

"The coordinates?" asked Adonis. Teekay
said the coordinates and Adonis entered
these in his watch.

"Something familiar about this place. I
have seen this before. Wait, a minute!"
said Teekay.

"I knew it! I have seen this before. Emma,
do you remember that day with our now
dead friend who thought he can subjugate
to everyone. Guess what? It's him dead as a
log," said Teekay cunningly.

"No. No. No. It wasn't him," shouted Emma.

"You want to bet? It's him. Douchebag is dead. Still not moving since that day," said Teekay bring that day's screen up.

"We all saw him got up and leave. What happened that day?" asked Jadanick.

"We have to go there right now," said Emma. Everyone left and headed to the lake. Natasha had planned to stay with Teekay from onward but the other girls insisted that she goes too with them. They drove for a while before they came to the lake. Most of them had landed here and left their spaceship somewhere in this lake. Adonis quickly activated a search mode and the search for missing Shane began. They all followed Adonis as he searched the area. This side of the lake signals were faint to be detected by his watch so they went to the other side. They finally detected the missing person. Jack quickly jumped into the lake. After a few minutes, he resurfaced to take a breath before going back inside the lake waters. More minutes later he came back with a watch. He gave them the watch and dived back into the lake waters. He kept on resurfacing to take a breath but he could not find anyone. Adonis joined in the search further down the lake that's when they found a body. They searched for his wallet or any identification. He was Shane born on the 25th of December from Antarctica. The girls started crying. Somehow, they felt responsible. It now made sense why the blonde man laughed so much after the fight. He had claimed one of them. They felt silly and cried inconsolable. A few days after burying Shane they were sitting in the lounge area talking.

"He could have been the answer to our problems. Everything here is written in Antarctic language," said Emma.

"What a shame we never had the chance to meet. Are we still going to be able to be the Emperor's bodyguards when one is missing? Everyone has a different role to play yet we are all mutually complementary."

"What was his role among us? Anyone knows?" asked Alina.

"Per his tattoo which was badly decomposing. He is the interpreter our tour guide if you like. He was the overseer or the fortune teller. The second ancient language is translated as; Staying together brings victory any loss rejuvenates evil to weaken you even further," said Emma. On hearing this there was a moment of silence. Everyone was now very afraid. Clearly, the loss of Shane had weakened them.

"There are no evils. The climate is the only evil threatening the survival of the Emperor," said Jack.

"I think you should know something guys," said Natasha looking at Sandra who in turn hugged Jadanick fearfully. She paused and cleared her throat.

"The night Adonis arrived I woke up in the middle of the night," she paused and breathed heavily.

"I couldn't sleep so I walked around the palace. I felt a bit cold and remembered that the room with the drums was one of the warmest in the house. I went in there," she stopped talking and looked down as if she wanted to cry.

"What did you see? Tell us Natasha," asked Adonis. "There were six animals each sleeping against the six of the seven drums," said Natasha. No one said anything for a while. "What kind of animals Natasha? Why you didn't tell us?" asked Alina.

"Two lions, one white, one brown, a leopard and a cougar," said Natasha.

"But you said six animals. You only mentioned four," asked Emma.

"I did not see clearly the other animals I froze with fear and walked out slowly," replied Natasha.

"Are you sure you were not dreaming? Why you didn't tell anyone or wake us up?" asked Alina.

"I was scared. I thought you might be in deep sleep and I would make noise and woken up the animals. That morning I told Sandra."

"Darling you knew this and never said anything to me?" asked Jadanick looking at Sandra who was hugging him tight.

"She told me. I just thought she wanted to

scare me because I wanted to stay and sleep that afternoon. I had not slept the night before you know," she said this raising her eyebrows at Jadanick.

"Ok. So, what do we do? If this is correct?" asked Emma.

"What do you me want should we do? It means we can't go back there again. Full stop," shouted Jadanick before continuing. "I will go with my Sandra to the new world if you do not want."

"Listen. We have been staying there for weeks now. Nothing happened and I do not think anything is going to happen to us. They must somehow belong to the Emperor if she wasn't dreaming," said Emma.

"Just a few minutes ago, you yourself you said that... wait a minute, let me quote you; Staying together brings victory any loss rejuvenates evil to weaken you even further. Now we lost one of us. So, what if evil try to weaken us?!" asked Jadanick.

"I understand what you are saying but I can also argue that Shane was dead for days if not weeks but nothing happened to us," explained Emma.

"Ok. But now you smell a dead person. Those animals, what if they start smelling us too? Look I am not trying to be funny you know. We were in close contact with a dead body. We might not detect it but our animal friends do. I am just saying we have to be careful," said Jadanick. Jack remained quiet he was only listening. This was a sensitive subject to him.

"Jay, the saying on the tattoo says also that if we stay together, we will be stronger. No matter where you go if evil wants you it will get you. We are better together," replied Alina. There was a moment of silence.

"The big question is that; what are we going to do about this?" asked Jack.

"We have to remain here. If the Emperor was here should we not be staying here as well? We are the chosen Emperor's bodyguards and we shall remain the same," said Emma.

"We need a plan. We must link all of us and synchronize each other so it's easy to know where you are and where you have gone. We will need to sleep in the same room. That includes you Jay and Sandra too no more getting jiggy. Okay?" asked Jack. They all agreed and for the first time they were afraid to go home early. They chose for the weather to caress them rather than be the meal of the hungry animals.

"What if the animals were the Emperor's bodyguards?" asked Alina.

"In that case, we have nothing to fear they are on our side," replied Adonis.

"Let's look at this from a different angle. What if the animals ate the Emperor? Where is the Emperor? What would stop them from eating the Emperor? With all due respect to Jack?" asked Jadanick.

"Highly unlikely I lived with my parents and friends all my life why I did not eat them?" asked Jack.

"Give the other watch to Natasha and show her how to use it. Jadanick and Sandra from today you should be one. Even if she goes to the toilet, go with her. Ok?" suggested Emma. Jadanick looked at Emma and then at Sandra before nodding in agreement.

"If you are in trouble, always touch your tattoo that activates the weapon and then use the watch, subjugate instantly that is the only way we are going to defeat evil," said Jack.

CHAPTER NINE

The next day they decided to search the
whole palace and all the rooms to make
sure that they were free from any animals.
They split into two groups Jadanick,
Sandra, Natasha and Jack went one way
and Emma, Alina and Adonis went the
other way. Emma, Alina and Adonis went
first in the room with the solar drums but
there was nothing. They came across a
room with a passage to another area of the
palace.

"What do you think?" asked Adonis
looking at the narrow small passage.

"The annoying fact is that you have to

crawl to the other side. What if there is danger there how quickly can we all get back?" asked Alina.

"Ok. I will go and check first. You two wait here," said Adonis. The two ladies nodded in agreement. Adonis knelt and crawled into the passage with a hand torch. Two minutes later he screamed aloud.

"What happened!? Are you okay?" asked Emma shouting and peeping through the hole to the passage. They can hear Adonis laughing his heart out.

"You are a jerk you know that?!" shouted Alina. The two ladies sat down and started talking.

"I am starting to think that probably the Emperor ran away. Just imagine living in this kind of weather. And if Natasha is right with all the kinds of threats. It must have been terrifying night after night," said Alina.

"I do not think it was that bad. He could not have spent a fortune building all this. I think that solar energy room has never been used before we are the first to actually use it," replied Emma.

"Did it ever occur to you that maybe the Emperor died? Surely, with all these daily commuting to the world above we should have met or heard something about him. He in fact might have died a long time ago and all these people we have asked do not know anything about him. I am just saying let's look at all the possibilities," pleaded Alina.

"Why would they send a spaceship for us if he is dead? That does not make any sense," asked Emma.

"See how easily Shane died. He did not even spend any time here. We have not even met him. He had no contact with the Emperor. He had not even seen the Emperor. He is in the same shoes as us so my question is what makes us different?" asked Alina playing with her watch.

"Listen Ali, do not be negative we have to be strong and stick to the plan it sounds like you are giving up hope," said Emma encouraging Alina who seemed unconvinced.

"Look at all this in this way. If Natasha is correct, then we can safely save the

Emperor as his bodyguards in the form of the animals. Right?" asked Alina.

"Right," replied Emma.

"So why then he need us. Ok if it's me I understand what about the rest. How come we dreamt about everything. We had visions before why are we not having visions now," asked Alina.

"Ladies I found something come to this side," shouted Adonis. Alina crawled first and went to the other side. Emma followed, and they all gathered on the other side. They saw a skeleton of a human being.

"Did the animals eat this person?" asked Alina.

"Highly unlikely if you ask me. Why? Because look at the body posture all bones are intact and he seemed like he died sitting down or leaning against the wall. If it was an animal attack, it could have been different," suggested Emma.

"I think I will agree with Emma. Animal attack highly unlikely. Death by natural cause or the weather," added Adonis.

"Ok. So, we can conclude that he died

when everyone had already gone. No one was left to bury him. That can also mean that the Emperor was already gone probably leaving these people here to starve to death or to be killed by the weather," explained Alina.

"Or he was a captured enemy left here to be eaten by the animals but the animals refused to eat him," said Emma trying to relieve the tension. They started walking toward the other rooms. They came across two skeletons one of a woman judging by the pelvis area and the other one of a young baby.

"All these people could not have died when the Emperor was here. The likely possible explanation is that he left but promised all these people to come back for them but never to return," explained Adonis.

"These people were loyal to the Emperor, they waited for him in vain. This could have been the warmest room in the palace. The narrow passage was to save energy from escaping. So, when the night falls women and children were brought in here at night to keep them warm but somehow still the night was too cold for comfort," explained Emma.

"What if they died of hunger?" asked Alina.

"Highly unlikely but still possible," replied Adonis. They kept walking ahead, and they came across a dark room. They looked for the lights and found them but the lights in that room were generally dim. This room looked like a room they kept and prepared dead bodies. There were slabs that looked like they were used as the first place they put dead bodies. They looked like coffins put on a shelf. The strange thing was that they had the same name which was just spelt differently. Adonis opened one of the coffin on the shelf and there was a skeleton of a baby inside. It was this time when Adonis' watch started beeping. Someone was asking for help. There was a message asking if he can accept to be used as a subjugating entity. He had less than ten seconds to acknowledge.

"Step back wait there far away from me. I do not know what is going to happen," shouted Adonis pushing the ladies to the other side. He accepted and waited thinking that maybe someone of them was being attacked. A few seconds later, the ladies saw a huge angry lion acting as if it wanted to attack them. They started running back the way they came from. Surely, they could not volunteer to be entities. They crawled back to the other side within a few minutes.

"Did you see that?" asked Emma. "Something is wrong. Let's go back and find the others to make sure that they are okay," said Alina. The two girls ran as fast as they can to the other side. There started shouting the other girls' names and Jadanick's. They came across Jadanick. "Something went wrong. Jack got scared by one of the animals and without knowing it he turned into one himself just before he subjugated. What happened is the opposite of what should have happened. The lion, has disappeared leaving his lifeless body lying there instead of the other way round. I had no option I thought the other lion was going to pounce on him. I just jumped toward the beast and the animal ran away. I carried jack, and he is in that room with the girls."

"Which room?" asked Alina just before a huge brown lion came out of that room he was pointing at.

"Oh, my god. What had just happened," asked Emma. Jadanick looked and saw the huge brown lion coming from the room where he had left Jack and the ladies?

"No no!"

Jadanick run after it and quickly entered the room he had left the ladies and Jack. The two ladies were in the corner hugging each other and Jack was lying on the floor.

"What happened!?" asked Jadanick. The two ladies just pointed at Jack.

"The lion came in after us but Jack stood in front of it, he collapsed and the lion just left," said Sandra.

"We have to leave as soon as possible. All you four stay here we will go and get Adonis," said Emma. Emma and Alina ran back to where they were before looking for Adonis. They went where they had left him before but he was not there.

"Adonis, where are you?" shouted Alina.

They looked around and saw some drag marks. They entered the room and heard some growling noises.

"It's Adonis," screamed Alina. He had been dragged into the room next door. Emma and Alina got his leg and dragged him outside. The lion followed him and when it saw Emma, it stood back and stopped at the door.

"We have to go," said Emma carrying Adonis together with Alina. They crawled through the narrow passage and went back where the others were. They all went back to the room they all were staying.

"We have to leave right now," said Natasha fearing for her life.

"I told you now you believe me. I can't stay here. If it wasn't for Jack, I might be dead by now. I will go to Teekay today," explained Natasha moving up and down the room.

"She has a point," replied Jadanick.

"So, what happened?" asked Emma.

"We heard a growling sound and before we know it Jack was on the floor while we attended to Jack we heard a growling sound just behind us. When we looked back, we saw this huge white lion looking at us. But as soon as it saw Jack it ran away. Soon after that Jack woke up we walked to the next room. I left, coming to you to tell you what had happened that's when we saw that big brown lion coming out of that room," added Jadanick.

"So, Jack is the answer to the animals. If he is on the floor, they won't attack but instead run away," hinted Emma.

"I am not taking any risks I know what you are implying," argued Natasha.

"Even if we go, we will end up dead because of the weather. I think we should try to find out a way of resolving this. If these animals were dangerous and after us nothing should have stopped them," added Alina.

"Myself and Sandra we are at risk. Every time the animals saw us they growled showing their teeth. I guess Jack and you guys are OK. We are not one of you so do not stop us. I am taking my things and I am leaving," shouted Natasha.

"Sandra, are you coming with me?" asked

Natasha. Sandra wanted to cry she did not know what to do. Natasha was right. For the first time in her life she has learned what fear really is. She looked at Jadanick. "Do not count on him. He left us. If it wasn't for Jack, we could have been mauled, to death. You saw it for yourself. Let's go," explained Natasha. Jadanick looked down at first knowing Natasha had a point. He had left just for a few seconds and that nearly cost her, her life.

"The decision is yours Darling. I am one of them and the animals also walked away from me," said Jadanick. There was a moment of silence.

"You do not get second chances in life. Let's go while we can," pleaded Natasha. Sandra got up and hugged Jadanick for a very long time. The two sobbed together, and they said goodbyes. They escorted them out of the building.

"Sandy, I love you babe," shouted Jadanick. The girls were already a few meters away bracing the cold weather going away. Jack, Alina, Adonis, Emma and Jadanick all watched them leave.

Sandra stopped and looked backward. She started running backward. Natasha could be heard saying no do not go back there. It seemed like it all happened in slow motion. Jadanick acted as if he was in a running competition. It looked like he was on the starting line and suddenly, the whistle was blown. Him being quicker than everyone else he just started running. In slow motion the two ran toward each other. They hugged each other and Jadanick lighted Sandra high into the air before bringing her down and giving her a smacker. They had their foreheads stuck together for a very long time. Natasha stopped and looked at them too. The two talked for some time and Sandra started going toward Natasha. She kept looking backward and blowing air-kisses to Jadanick. Moments later she disappeared with Natasha. The rest of the group entered inside the building without waiting for Jadanick. He followed them inside the building too. "What if the Emperor is dead and these animals they are guarding him now? Should we not follow them to find out as they pose no danger to us?" asked Emma. They all looked at each other. It was a sad notion to even think about. They waited for a very long time for them to protect and serve the Emperor.

"I think Emma has a point we should follow the animals," said Adonis. They all agreed. This was the only explanation that made sense. They waited for the animals to come to the room with the solar drums but for days the animals didn't turn up. The following days they planned to search for the animals further down the unused buildings of the former Emperors' palace. The search began and this time they went further to the old unused buildings. They took hand torch lights and fluorescent lighters. After sometime they heard some growling noises. They walked toward where the noise was coming from. They reached a place where all the animals were gathered. Fear struck in all of them. The first thing that came in their mind was that the Emperor was dead. They looked around where the animals were and it seemed there were guarding something.

"What is the plan? I think if the animals are guarding something and if we approach there could be a danger to us," said Alina.

"Maybe let Jack approach them and see what happens," asked Emma.

They all looked at Jack as he slowly made strides ahead. As he approached, the lions stood up and looked at him. They started making threatening sounds as he approached. He looked down where the other animals were. He saw that they were all sitting around something. He looked clearly and saw what appeared to be a skeleton. That freaked him out and for some reason the animals sensed fear in him and they got up and advanced forward ready to attack. Jack suddenly slumped to the ground and a third lion came from nowhere and it stood in front of Jack. The animals started fighting, the two lions and the other one that came out of Jack. Suddenly all the animals started chasing the new lion which ran in a different direction. They all touched Jack, and he woke up. They walked toward the place the animals were guarding. They saw a skeleton. The animals all slept around the skeleton.

"So, is this the Emperor?" asked Jadanick No one answered they all sat down.

"This is the only thing that makes sense," added Jadanick.

"What do you me?" asked Alina

"This is our mission to preserve the bloodline of the Emperor," replied Jadanick.

"We have to think like the animals," continued Jadanick.

"This can't be. All the way from Moscow to guard bones?" asked Emma in shock.

"This could be the new meaning of protecting the Emperor," said Adonis.

"If he is dead, why do we need to protect him. Protecting him from who?" asked Jack.

"He is already dead. If he was alive, maybe it was to protect him from the animals," said Alina

"Maybe to honor him and to serve him means to give him a proper burial," said Emma sitting down.

"You are right. Our mission is to find the Emperor and give him a proper burial. The animals had guarded him so nothing bad happened to his bones," said Jack.

"It makes sense. Emperors needed proper burial for them to continue their life in after life," added Alina.

"I have a question if our duty like every magnificent warrior is to protect him and his bloodline, to guaranteed the continued ruling of the Emperor's bloodline what part is linked to that if we are just to bury him?" asked Emma.

"What are you inferring to?" asked Jack.

"Look, maybe we do not need just to bury him. Maybe we are to collect his DNA and find his bloodline. They can't ask for the young Emperor's bodyguards if it was simply to bury him," remarked Emma.

"She is right burial is performed by priests only. If it was just to bury him, they could have sent a priest. Anyone here from a priestly background?" asked Adonis.

"No," they all replied.

"So, you are saying we must take his bones and find his DNA and then try to trace his bloodline and then protect them?" asked Alina.

"Correct. I think that's the only explanation that makes sense so far," replied Emma.

"I think I understand everything now. The weather has posed a real threat to the survival of the Emperor's bloodline. I think probably he died because of the cold weather. The urgency arose from the fact that the sudden temperature changes would destroy DNA thereby making it hard to trace his bloodline," paused Jack.

"Imagine during the day temperatures reaching up to 30 to 40 'C and at night temperatures dropping to minus 20 to 40'C surely this will destroy the DNA. So, we are here to search for the Emperor's bloodline. To do that what do we need?" asked Jack not expecting a reply.

"The Emperor's DNA. The animals were protecting him now it is our turn to get his DNA and bury him and look for his bloodline," said Jack before sitting down. That gave everyone hope. That is what everyone wanted to hear. The dream was alive. This was a challenging mission. The world has changed and the Emperor's bodyguards had not changed nor evolved. There were new threats to the survival of the Emperor.

"I think I understand this now more than before," added Adonis.

"Look! A long time ago the main threats to the survival of the Emperor's bloodline were from man and animals. So animals were the perfect protection weapons. Nowadays the weather has changed and the threats are no longer just animals. The weapons have changed to look at Alina. Her duty is to provide the much-needed sun. Look with technological development Emma is to jam all the signals thereby ensuring the survival of the bloodline of the Emperor," added Adonis.

"Today we have a greater role to play. We must preserve the Emperor's DNA from the hostile weather. We get his DNA and we will try to locate his blood relative and preserve him," said Adonis. The animals didn't come back it seemed like a change after all. The animals had done their role in protecting the Emperor's bones until the magnificent warriors had arrived to take over. Adonis and Jack went back to the other place where they had seen a big box enough to put the Emperor's bones. They gathered around and prepared to take his bones. The bottom half of the skeleton was covered in soil, slowly they dug him out.

"It's a woman!" shouted Jadanick .

"What?" asked Emma.

"He is right it's a woman," replied Alina.

"Look at the pelvis the shape is that of a woman," added Jadanick.

"So where is the Emperor?" asked Jack.

"It's good news this still keep our hopes alive," added Adonis .

"So why the Emperor's bodyguards are guarding a woman?" asked Adonis.

"Probably guarding the Emperor's wife," replied Jadanick.

"Highly unlikely. The Emperor's bodyguards protects only the Emperor or his sons and not his wife," replied Emma.

"Ok maybe she was pregnant with his son. That could explain why the animals were guarding her," said Jadanick.

"Yes," they shouted all at once pointing at Jadanick.

"The Emperor's wife was pregnant, and the Emperor left her to die alone here. I do not think so," said Emma.

"What if he asked her to wait for him here? Probably it was too dangerous for the wife and the baby to venture outside. He asks them to wait for him here. He leaves his guards protecting her in the form of the animals. He is planning to come back, but he fails to come back. She waits for him and dies of cold weather or hunger," said Alina.

"Very good that makes sense," said Jack.

"Or that the Emperor leaves her not knowing that she was pregnant but the animals will still protect her then tragically she dies," added Jadanick.

"Still a good explanation and a possibility," said Emma.

"So, now our duty from now on is to look for the bones of the Emperor and preserve his bloodline through the use of DNA. After that we will try to locate his closest bloodline and protect him. Until we are sure that he is alive I think we should concentrate in finding where he died and take his DNA," said Emma.

CHAPTER TEN

A few weeks after the day they discovered the skeleton of the presumed Emperor's wife. The animals left the Emperor's palace and not to be seen again. The whole group went to Teekay to try to find out the meaning of Jadanick's tattoo.

"Can you copy and redraw this tattoo on your computer? We want to know the meaning of this?" asked Emma. Jadanick was very excited to see his girlfriend it seemed things were okay now, and he hinted that it was okay for her to come back if she wanted. Teekay did not hesitate soon he was doing what he does best. He wrote everything down and brought everything on the screen. Some of it was some verb like messages written in what they found out to be a primitive Chinese.

"Looking at the big picture this is some kind of map. After trying to find out what some symbols meant they found out that this was like a plan to build an empire or palace or kingdom if you want to call it," said Teekay.

"Can you get the plan of the complex and the city gate and compare them with this one? I have a feeling this plan on Jay's back refers to that place," suggested Emma.

"I will see what I can do," replied Teekay. He quickly searched for the map of the city gate to compare with.

"If you can. Can you please get the map before the construction of the city gate too?" asked Alina.

"If it still exists yes, I will get one," replied Teekay.

"So, did you find the Emperor?" asked Natasha.

"We are still searching. I think probably

your mission is to get his DNA and then find his bloodline," replied Adonis.

"The map I think it matches the one before construction more than it does with the modern map," replied Teekay.

"It seems there is a river of some kind flowing across the map whereas on the map before and after construction there seems to be a lake in the middle of the map," added Teekay.

"I have entered some symbols on the translation panel in the search engine and three of them refer to his resting place. I think you must look at this," said Teekay pointing at the places on the map. One place stood prominent to everyone because they had seen the place before. It was a place where they have seen the skeleton of the female. The place the animals slept and spent most of their time.

"The saying is that Emperors normally get buried with their bodyguards, family, priest and everyone close to them normal at the same place, same graveyard," said Jack.

"So, having that in mind we assume we

have found his wife and so we must look for him in the same place," added Jack

"What are the other two places?" asked Emma.

"The first one I think could be a mistake or some kind. This place I have shifted the map a few degrees off but still it still points to one place. The place is in the water, in the river, or lake," replied Teekay.

"In the lake? Never heard of that before and highly unlikely. Impossible, I guess," replied Adonis. They all kept silent for a while pondering the possibility but soon dismissed the idea. They all agreed with Adonis.

"The third place is a place used to be in the garden of the palace. The place is outside the complex on a hilly slope that used to house a waterfall of the smaller part of the river. On the new map this is one of the beauty landscape outside the complex," replied Teekay.

"I think our best option is back to the palace near where we found the Emperor's wife," said Emma. They all went back to the Emperor's old palace. Teekay even volunteered to go as well with them bringing with him his state-of-the- art equipment to try to help locate the missing Emperor. They didn't waste time soon they were on their task. They went to that place where they found the skeleton of the Emperor's wife. They looked for any skeletons and any hints to his whereabouts but there was none. The following day they went to the second place outside in the open air near the waterfall. Suddenly Emma collapsed, and she was in and out of trances. For the first time since they arrived her eyes changed in front of everyone. One eye remained blue and the other one turned green. She started acting like she was possessed. She started chanting. Several times she kept repeating these words; Through her everything is possible for she can see in this world and in the world of the gods for no one is like her. They stopped searching for the bones of the Emperor. They returned home with Emma. She was hallucinating as well. They stayed with her hoping that out of this they will be able to find the Emperor. A few days passed when she was still like that. Then one night they were all asleep when she screamed and then she walked out staggering going in the direction where they were to search for the Emperor.

"Darling wake up! Something is wrong with Emma. She just went outside. We have to follow her," said Sandra.

They all got up and started following in the direction she had gone. She came to this small tree near the road to the waterfall and she fell. She stood up and continued running. She came to this place near the waterfall and sat on the ground. For some time, she fell asleep. She woke up when she heard Alina's voice shouting her name. Alina soon came to find her sat there.

"Emma, Alina," shouted Jadanick looking for the two ladies.

"There they are," shouted Adonis. They both went in the direction where the ladies were. They all arrived there and when Emma saw Jadanick she started screaming and shouting.

"He wants to kill me. He is trying to kill me," shouted Emma pointing at Jadanick.

She looked really frighten.

"No. Emma. This is Jadanick. He is one of us," explained Alina holding Emma in her arms.

"She is hallucinating," added Jack.

"Get me back in the house before he kills me please my sister," said Emma begging Alina. Alina lifted Emma and took her back where they were staying.

"I do not know what is going on but I do not like how this sounds," explained Jadanick.

"Do not worry man. She is hallucinating she is not saying you want to kill her. She is re-living another person's life," replied Adonis.

"So, are you saying in that other life there was someone who looked like me?" asked Jadanick pacing up and down the room.

"What I do not understand is that why did she not say you or Adonis. Why me? What do you think my girlfriend will think about all this? We just got back together," explained Jadanick.

"Look Jadanick it is more like this. Take modern synchronizing for example. The person can easily track your movements the same was as going into another life in the past. She is now synchronized with a girl in the past life. It just happened now she is re-living that life. So, nothing to worry about even your girlfriend will understand that this is not happening right now, but it is just a flashback," explained Jack.

"So why would one of them try to kill her?" asked Sandra.

"If Jadanick represented someone during her days, why would he try to kill her," added Sandra.

"I do not think he was one of them," added Alina.

"The fear on Emma's face says it all, it also means this person was ruthless and above all the previous centuries they were either all boys or all girls. Only this century when we are mixed boys and girls," explained Alina.

"Why would he try to kill her," asked Jadanick.

"First question we should ask I think is what kind of relationship was there between them?" said Jack.

"Maybe he was just a stranger," replied Natasha.

"Highly unlikely because her sister knew that person. Her sister was not afraid of him. I think it can fall in the category of a family member or close relative," said Adonis.

"She was an Emperor's bodyguard. So, the likely person was the Emperor himself. He is the only person she was capable of being afraid of," said Alina. They all looked at each other and then they all looked at Jadanick.

"Why are you all staring at me like that, as if you have seen a ghost?" asked Jadanick.

"I do not get you?" remarked Jadanick.

"Are you saying that the Emperor himself is the one trying to kill his own bodyguards?" asked Jadanick.

"We are starting to think so?" replied Alina.

"I was going through the diary Emma was reading, which was written by a student at a university in China. He swore that the Emperor for some reasons unknown to him had broken the rules," said Alina.

"So, he might have broken the rules so what? He is the Emperor," said Jadanick.

"The rules I think he was talking about are the sacred rules," replied Alina.

"Which sacred rules?" asked Adonis.

"To protect the Emperor properly. There were rules that were put in place. These aimed to preserve the tradition and relationship between Emperors and the magnificent bodyguards. For example, the Emperor was not allowed at any point in his life to enter the room with the magic stones," remarked Alina.

"By entering the room meant breaking the oath and jeopardizing the safety of the magnificent warriors. This is because entering the room would enable the linked with the magnificent warriors. Which confused them," replied Alina.

"To add more to that I would like to say that he was like the magnificent warriors in that he had a tattoo and a weapon as well. Him being the center link he had more power than all combined," said Jack.

"So, are you saying that if he wanted, he

didn't need the magnificent warriors?" asked Jadanick.

"Exactly!" replied Adonis.

"Only the Emperor could absorb all their energies and render their weapons useless. If he wanted to be greedy, he would take all the weapons for himself. This is true in that in the end if all the magnificent warriors died all the weapons will stay with the Emperor instead of going to the new warriors," explained Jack.

"So, all these seven animals Natasha saw in the room with the solar drums. They represent the previous magnificent warriors?" asked Sandra.

"Yes," replied Alina.

"So why kill the people who are protecting you?" asked Natasha.

"Several reasons. The magnificent warriors lived by rules and morals. Imagine having the ability to rule the world? To take whatever you want at will. What would stop you if you were the Emperor?" asked Alina looking at everyone in turn.

"No one. No one can stop you if you are the

Emperor," replied Jadanick.

"Wrong. The warriors had more powers than the Emperor but this was never publicized. The warriors had powers to prevent the Emperor from becoming greedy and self-centered. There were their moderators. They advised the Emperor on which course of action to take after considering, morals and society at large. They represented the people. They stopped the Emperors from being greedy and from bending the rules to suit them. Imagine that the Emperor wanted someone's wife for himself. Morally it was forbidden but he could easily let the warriors kill the husband so that he takes his wife. So, the warriors were there to stop things like this," said Alina.

"I understand that the last Emperor was the richest of all the Emperors and why does that not surprise me. Especially considering the fact that they said that he broke the rules and entered the room with the magic stones," said Jack.

"So, if he had the power to disable the powers of the warriors why not just take the powers and let them go? Why kill them?" asked Sandra.

"That's a very good question I was just thinking about that," said Jack.

"I think I know the answer to that," said Alina before she proceeded talking.

"We and all the magnificent warriors are warriors to protect the Emperor forever so the weapon and powers we have will never leave us unless only when we are dead. The Emperor no matter what when we are alive cannot fully take the powers. This is the reason he must kill. Once the warrior is dead, then the powers belonged to the Emperor," said Alina.

"Damn that's so cruel, you sacrificed a lot to come and serve him and protect him yet he is the one ending your life," said Natasha. They were talking when Emma screamed from the bedroom. They all rushed in there to find what was going on. She had her eyes wide opened as if someone who has seen a ghost. She screamed and later acted like she was failing to breathe.

"Nick," and her eyes' color changed to

brown, and she fell into a trance. She slept the whole day until the next day. After that it seemed she was okay everything was back to normal. She seemed not to remember anything that happened. One day the whole group left the palace of the Emperor and went to the city. They left Teekay and Natasha.

"What do you want to do today Natasha babe," asked Teekay.

"Spend some time with you and have the whole day to ourselves Emperor," said Natasha.

"Emperor woo! You know how to get me in the mood babe," replied Teekay.

"Anything for my man, we have been through a lot now it's just you and me. Let's enjoy the day before they come back," said Natasha. Natasha and Teekay had become very close after the day she found the animals sleeping in the room with the solar drums. She realized that life is short. Why not enjoy life? All her life she had waited for a perfect man and honestly, she would not look at Teekay twice. Teekay was small and mean. He thought he was the god himself. He used to drink a lot. He seemed never to understand women. He had spent most of his days on the computer desk. Natasha did not that. She wanted someone who was spontaneous and dynamic. Someone full of life and one who was adventurous and rich too. It seemed this episode had benefited Teekay more than Natasha. She had realized that it was better to enjoy life as Mr. perfect might never come on time. They cuddled the whole afternoon. It was warm for some time they chose to take a nap outside. They woke up to find themselves surrounded by seven animals. The lion got really agitated and started walking toward Teekay. The white one and the brown one grabbed Teekay and mauled him to the horror of Natasha. He fought back as much he could, but he was outnumbered. They just mauled him and watched him bleed to death. Natasha quickly remembered what they had taught her. She quickly opted to subjugate. "Come on please hurry," she said looking at her watch. Adonis was with the rest of

the group in the city when his watch beeped. He looked at his watch and stayed behind for a while scrolling down.
He only said.
"Natasha what is wrong," before he screamed and fell to the ground. He was bleeding his thigh was mauled, and he appeared to being dragged by something. Everyone ran to his rescue and quickly opted to subjugate back to Natasha. There was no point for Natasha to subjugate if it was an animal attack you will only be getting everyone injured. This is the main reason why magnificent warriors had animal weapons. Animals once they have initiated an attack will not leave you until you are dead or incapacitated. They quickly rushed him to the hospital while the others headed back home. Jack, Alina and Emma went back home to Natasha's rescue and Jadanick and Sandra went to the hospital with Adonis. The time Jack, Alina and Emma arrived back home, Teekay was dead. There was blood everywhere. It seemed that the animals were not interested in Teekay. They just

mauled him and left him to die. They took Natasha with them. They looked everywhere hoping to find her probably mauled to death, but she was not there. Quickly they searched her through her watch and started tracking her. The trail led them to a place outside the city. It was getting dark.

"Let's stop and talk about this first," said Emma.

"It's dark and what are we trying to do?" she continued.

"Rescue Natasha. I do not think she is dead. These animals they do not carry anyone. If they are hungry, they just kill and eat there. If they want just to kill, they kill and leave the person there. This is out of character. They do not drag someone and then take her somewhere, that just not animal behavior," said Jack feeling upset.

"Maybe they have young ones and they are bringing them food," said Alina.

"Stop talking like that. She is one of us. I say we must find her. She risked her life trying to help us. I say we continue to look for her until we are sure that she is dead," suggested Jack. They continued searching for Natasha. Her watch was still on. They kept following the trail. They were surprised by how far the animals had traveled.

"Wait a minute I know this place," said Jack stopping to look at his watch.

"The first time I arrived I came through this place," said Jack.

"If you ask me honestly, I do not know where we are right now," said Emma.

"If memory serves me right my spaceship is not far away from here. We are near the lake. We better hurry," said Jack before they started running again. They reached the lake and shouted her name.

"Natasha, where are you?" shouted Jack.

"Let's spread out. You go that way. I go that way and you look around here," said Jack. They all separated and started looking for Natasha. They all stopped and activated the search mode, that is, when they heard something falling into the lake water. They looked ahead that's when they saw the animals all running away. They all ran as fast as they can toward the place where Natasha had been thrown into the lake waters. Jack jumped into the water first followed by Emma and then by Alina. Natasha was still alive, but she had her leg badly mauled. She had lost a lot of blood. It was a frantic race to try to save her. They managed to stop the bleeding. She was in and out of unconscious. Jack went back into the lake water and started his spaceship. He was about to fly Natasha to the hospital when Emma stood up leaving her lying there next to the lake lifeless. They all wept uncontrollably.

CHAPTER ELEVEN

Some time weeks after the Natasha incident, Emma, Alina Jadanick, Sandra, Adonis and Jack were all in the library researching.

"Still up to today I still do not understand why the animals dragged Natasha from the palace to the lake?" said Emma looking at Alina.

"I initially thought that they had young curbs, and they wanted food for their young ones but this was just out of character," replied Alina.

"When we arrived, it seemed they were waiting for us to arrive. Or that we scared these animals," added Emma.

"It seemed as if they threw her into the lake waters. Which is bizarre," said Alina?

"It seems there is something strange about this lake. We found Shane too in this lake. Correct?" asked Adonis.

"Yes. He drowned there too," replied Jack before he continued talking.

"I, myself since the day I first arrived there his was my destination. I arrived there thinking that this is where I was to find the Emperor. I have been coming to this place ever since mainly because I left my spaceship here but sometimes I felt really connected to this place," explained Jack.

"Strangely If I remembered correctly this place is one of the places mentioned on Jadanick's tattoo as his resting place. So much has gone on here to just ignore that. Let's see what we know about this place. They scrolled on the e-books and tablets in the library searching for any information they can get.

"The lake was formerly a river per this article," said Adonis.

"But during the construction they filled the lower and upper rivers to save water and make this a lake and apart from that there is nothing special about this lake," explained Jack.

"It's popular with visitors because it the only safest landing site. I bet Adonis will second that," said Alina.

"That's correct do you think if I had landed here I could have suffered such injuries?" asked Adonis.

"Maybe we all need to go to that lake and spend the day there," said Emma.

"We have to sometime in the future," replied Jack.

"Wait, a minute. Guys, come and see this. I have found part of the legend which that Chinese student used to write notes in the diary," shouted Emma.

"It's written that Emperors, are to be protected forever and their bloodline preserved and they are to be honored in this life and in after life. Which we all know," said Emma.

"Here is the interesting part. It reads that whenever an Emperor dies before his time priests will come and take over from that period until the end," said Emma.

"So, it seems priest play a crucial role too. I thought that say when the Emperor dies first the magnificent warriors will take over," said Jadanick.

"No. They have no authority to rule, their role was solely to protect and serve the Emperor," replied Jack.

"The legend went on to say that whenever the Emperor dies, he shall be buried on land and his tomb made sacred and holy. All his servants and bodyguards who die after him shall be buried next to him so that in after life they shall be together again," read Emma.

"If all his servants and bodyguards when they die they are to be buried next to him why is it difficult for us to find where he was buried?" asked Emma.

"We have not been looking that much I think we should search again this weekend. What do you think?" asked Adonis.

"Are you strong enough to walk for long distances?" asked Jack.

"Yes sure. Since the day, they removed the stitches I feel great," replied Adonis.

"Ok let's search again this weekend. Ok guys?" asked Emma.

"The other interesting passage is in regard to the burial ceremony after his death. The passage reads: After his death and after a passage of time more than 15 years the Emperor if not properly buried or washed by the priests then he shall be given a ceremonial burial and be united with his precious possessions to prepare him for afterlife.

"Can someone explain what this means," asked Sandra.

"When an Emperor dies, and he is not given a proper burial, then after 15 years the priest must hold a ceremony to link his possession with him and prepare him for afterlife," replied Jadanick.

"What do you mean possessions? Does this include his magnificent warriors too? That's what I am asking you," said Sandra. No one replied her everyone looked down.

"So, why are you all ignoring me? What are you hiding? You must tell me the truth. So, I know what is going on," shouted Sandra.

"Yes. His bodyguards must also be united with him and prepare for the after life," replied Emma.

"So. Darling does that mean you are going to die? Are you going to be united with the Emperor?" asked Sandra feeling sad.

"No Darling it's not use. We were not his bodyguards. He had his own bodyguards I think they all died too. The animals now represent them. So, the animals will die and somehow get reunited with the former bodyguards. So, don't you worry. Okay?" asked Jadanick.

"Okay babe," replied Sandra.

"So, it seems it's that time to link the Emperor with his possessions. It seems he died more than 15 years ago. That could explain why we did not start at the age of seven. There was no Emperor. That could also mean that he had no bloodline in the form of a son. Our mission is to find him and give him a proper burial and link him with his possession. Maybe after that the seven animals will go too," explained Alina. For the first time that is the only explanation that made sense. All the other explanations did not make any sense at all. That gave more meaning to their mission.

"Ok this is the frightening passage from the legend and it reads; Just before the end there shall be a period of cleansing which initiates the beginning of the end which shall be marked by the spillage of blood on the surface of the land where the Emperor shall be buried and where all his possessions shall be placed in the earth to prepare him for afterlife.

"Does this ring a bell? Anyone?" asked Emma.

"They all raised up their hands," apart from Adonis.

"I think this is what happened that day when Teekay died," said Emma before she continued talking.

"I remembered all of us questioning what happened that day. Here is the answer."

"So, shouldn't we be very afraid of all this?" asked Jadanick.

"At least we know where to bury him and put all his stuff," answered Alina.

"I think we all have to be afraid but at least slowly we are starting to understand what is going on," replied Jack. The next weekend they all gathered where Teekay had died and performed rituals as they have read in the library. After that they decided to go and search where the Emperor might have been buried. They first took flowers to put on Shane's, Teekay and on Natasha's graves. The whole area was the most likely place where more people can be buried in one area. The day was a bit hot than most of the days. Jadanick drove them in his car.

"What do you think guys? When all this is over. I think we should go on a picnic. What do you say to that?" asked Alina.

"Sure, when we have time why not. Since we arrived here, we never got any spare time. Its mystery after mystery sometimes you just need to enjoy life," replied Sandra. They drove for a while and after some time they arrived at the gate to the burial place. They got out of the car and started walking toward the place they had buried Teekay first, which was close to the entrance on the left side. They laid flowers on his grave and talked about him. They joked about him, how funny he looked and how much he meant to Natasha. After they finished they went to the area where they had buried. Shane.

"Ah oh my god!! He is gone! Shane is gone!" screamed Alina.

"What happened?" asked Adonis running toward Alina who had gone to Shane's grave first.

"Someone dug him out. Look! He is gone," shouted Alina Everyone gathered on Shane's grave.

"Emma is this in the legend too that someone comes and dug him out of the grave?" asked Alina shocked and upset about all this.

"Wait, a minute," said Jack kneeling down. He looked on and around the grave. "Why do we have an animal's paws and prints everywhere?" asked Jack. They all gathered together to see what he meant, they all knelt down. Surely it must have been the animals. Their paws were everywhere.

"Honestly I have never seen anything like this before. Are they after food or what?" asked Sandra.

"Food I doubt it. These animals eat fresh meat only with blood. Shane had been gone for a long time so food is out of the question," replied Jadanick.

"So why then?" asked Adonis.

"Several reasons. The main one being that they are telling us that we have buried him in the wrong place so I think now he is home at that other place where Teekay died," explained Emma. What we can do is to try to look for him. If it's the animals for sure, then they might have just left him anywhere near here. The group went altogether around the graveyard looking for Shane in case the animals abandoned him somewhere nearby. But they couldn't find him.

"Do not move! Do not say a thing. Look ahead of you on Natasha's grave," said Jadanick holding Emma's hand. Everyone stopped and looked ahead of them.

"Do not move everyone stay where you are until I say so," whispered Emma. The animals all lay across Natasha's grave. All seven animals were all on Natasha's grave. That freaked all of them. How often do you see something like this? This was more than a coincidence so they thought.

"Jack, you will be in control. Tell us how best to deal with this situation."

"I cannot wait I have to go, last time he fainted we nearly got killed," said Sandra running for it.

"Babe stopped right there. If the animals sense your fear they will attack you. Please Darling wait. The animals do not just kill. They kill for a reason. To explain things to use. They were the Emperors," pleaded Jadanick. One of the lion the brown one stood up and looked at Sandra who quickly came back to Jadanick and the others. They slowly altogether as a group started moving backward slowly but facing the animals. The white lion stood up too and started walking toward them. They froze for a while. It raised its head and raised its neck hairs. It stopped and looked at everyone.

"Quickly turn around and start walking away do not run," said Jack after noticing that they were too close and that made it feel threatened. They reached the gate and looked backward. The animals weren't following them. They entered the car all of them.

"Damn! That was close," remarked Jadanick pausing for a while shaking his head.

"Honestly, I do not want to be in a situation like that again, ever."

"There are so many questions that remained unanswered. every day, we get more questions than answers," explained Jack.

"First Shane's body is missing and second, they are on Natasha's grave. Is this a coincidence?" asked Adonis.

"Can someone explain why all on Natasha's grave?" asked Alina.

"First it can be a way of re-living the kill. Mainly it's the leader's idea presumably the white lion. He wants to assert authority by showing what they will all end up like. Secondly it could be just because she is the recent person to be buried here therefore she is still fresh. When hunger strikes, this is the person they can dig and eat. Third, they share a connection with her maybe through the Emperor we just do not know it. Fourth just a mere coincidence," replied Emma.

"What about Shane?" asked Sandra.

"I think Shane's case will shade a lot of light on our mission. Shane can be used to represent the Emperor. Shane is in the wrong place. He was buried at the wrong place and our mission is to bury Shane again somewhere not here. He must be buried somewhere safe. Somewhere where he is close to the Emperor," replied Jack. They all keep quiet for some time.

"I think the animals took Shane to that place near the palace where it is said is the burial place of the Emperor. I think we should follow the animals and see where they are going they can give us some hints about the whereabouts of the Emperor," said Adonis.

"I think we should all go home. He could

have been left near home."

"I think Adonis has a point. We should all follow the animals and see where they are going," said Jack. While they were still parked there, a leopard came and jumped on top of the car and sat there for some time before the other animals started walking away. All the animals came toward them. They stood in front of them and the leopard jumped from the rooftop and they all left.

"Let's follow the animals first and see where they are going," asked Jack.

"I think we have had enough mishap for one day. Let's go home we can follow the animals some other day," replied Emma. After the animal's left they all decided to go home to the palace. The journey back home was the quietest they had ever had. No one said anything to anyone. The sound of the engine was the only sound they heard on their way home. They arrived home with much anticipation and to Emma's dismay there was no Shane's body there. If she had listened to Jack, they could have been led to the correct place for where the Emperor was buried. The following morning, they started to dig a big grave where Teekay's blood had been spilled. They dug a big hole and started putting some staff they found in the cabinet that belonged to the Emperor. They could not locate the Emperors bones so they waited and continued with the search. One weekend they went to the lake to have a picnic there.

"It seemed like a good day today. I think this is the best for everyone a time to wind down," said Alina.

"Surely it has been a long time coming. Everyone deserves that here and there." They had just parked the car nearby when a group of vultures flew to the air from the other side of the lake. That's seemed a little odd for Jadanick.

"A group of vultures? That seems very odd?" said Jadanick.

"Probably the only water source out here. I can't blame them today it has been a hot day I need something to drink too," said Adonis. They took everything they needed and sat next to the lake. They had food and drinks before the vultures returned and this time they were fighting before flying up again and returning a few seconds later. This was odd. Jack quickly rose and stood there for a few minutes before cursing. "Damn! Something is there. It's not just the water they are after." They all stood up and started walking toward that place. When they were near the vultures, the vultures flew a few meters in ahead of them. As soon as Jack discovered that they were feasting on a human carcass he whistled and clapped his hands then the vultures flew away and landed a few meters ahead of them.

"Oh, my god! It's Shane look at the clothes. I can't believe it all the way from the graveyard." Replied Jack.

"There is something strange going on and whatever it is I am starting not to like this," said Adonis.

"The animals dug Shane up only to bring him here? That does not make any sense," said Alina. Can someone explain what is going on?" asked Sandra.

"The animals dug up Shane so that they

can feed the vultures? Anybody help?" asked Emma. Honestly no one really knows what was going on. Initially the lake was Shane's resting place. They had found him in there.

"What do we do now? Should we take him back to the graveyard and burying him again or leave him here?" asked Emma.

"I think if we take him to the graveyard if the animals do not want him there they might dig him up again," said Adonis.

"Let's take him home and put him in the grave we dug," said Alina. They took the blankets they had brought for the picnic and rolled whatever was left of him and put him in the car. They headed back home to the palace. They drove for a while before they noticed the animals following the car.!

"OMG! Look! Behind," Shouted Sandra.

"What is it? What is going on," asked Jadanick who continued driving?

"The animals are following us. Look one, two, three, four, all seven of them," shouted Adonis.

"What shall we do?" asked Alina.

"Stop the car for a while. Please make sure that all the doors are locked and that all the windows are closed. Ok?", shouted Emma. Everyone checked the doors and the windows making sure that the windows and doors were all closed. Jadanick moved to the right side and parked the car on the right side. They stopped and waited.

"We might as well find out what they want now than to invite them home without knowing what they are after," explained Emma.

"Good idea," replied Jack. They waited for the animals to arrive. First was the white lion, followed by the brown lion, and then another lion then the leopard, then the cougar, then the cheetah side by side with the tiger. The animals stopped, and all surrounded the car. They circled the car rubbing against each other before they all lay down in turns. This time the tiger took the lead. Followed by the lion and then the other lion. The third lion lay down after and then the leopard, then the cheetah and lastly the cougar.

"That's strange, can anyone explain what is going on?" asked Sandra.

"It seemed that the animals slept forming a circle around the car. Is this the way they guard dead people, first the Emperor's wife and then Shane," said Alina.

"Maybe they are guarding us," said Adonis.

"I do not think so if it was us they could be sleeping outside the palace but instead they ran away first day they met a new lion friend thanks to Jack," replied Emma.

"Strange guys. We are seven and the animals are seven too. For the first time, we have matched them and they are now guarding us," said Jadanick.

"It seems they cannot guard us unless if we match them, one for each of them," replied Alina.

"Is this supposed to mean something," asked Jack. Emma quickly took out the diary and started reading it.

"I think I saw the passage that explains the bringing together of everyone. She flipped the pages of the diary as fast as she can, searching for the passage. After sometime she found the passage.

"It reads; She is the one that brings them together, she is the link and only through her shall they find their way. For she is special for only here can see this world and the world of the gods.

"I have no idea. Not sure what the link here is?" replied Adonis.

"The tiger," said Sandra.

"So, you think the tiger is the link. Why?" asked Jadanick.

"For the first time, it took the lead," replied Sandra.

"I would say the cougar. Because it sat last there by completing the link so it is the link," replied Jack.

"I think Jack is right," the cougar completes the circle so it can be the link. replied Emma.

"So, guys what are we going to do," asked Sandra as outside started getting dark.

"Let's go to the palace," replied Jadanick. Jadanick switched on the car lights and sounded the horn and the animals stood up. They drove off going to the palace. The animals did not stop following them.

"They are still following," said Sandra.

They all looked backward through the windows.

"Nothing to worry about I think we will be OK," replied Emma. They arrived home and got out of the car and put Shane in one of the graves they had dug outside. They waited in the car to see if the animals will stay with them or with Shane. The animals didn't turn up. For some reason, they stopped following and went back. It was getting cold and everyone went inside.

"It seems there is still something wrong. But I guess this the way it should be. We guarding the Emperor and the animals are now protecting us. At least that is how it was centuries ago," explained Alina.

"The animals are guarding us but we are not guarding the Emperor. If the Emperor was here why the animals didn't spend the night here? They sleep wherever the Emperor is. If we had tried to track the animals down at night, we should have known by now where the Emperor is," replied Jack.

"Tomorrow we should try to find out the movements of the animals. We should drive around until we know for sure where they sleep. It's too late tonight, and we are exhausted," said Jack. They agreed to start following the animals. They all slept. In the morning, they woke up to find that Shane had gone.

CHAPTER TWELVE

"Darling can we talk?" asked Sandra.
"Yes of course Darling," replied Jadanick.
"I want you to know that I love you so
much. Whatever decision I am going to
make has nothing to do with us. Last night
I understood this more than I had before.
Even though I love you so much we are not
meant to be together," paused Sandra
wiping tears from her cheeks.
"Do not say that. You know we belong,"
replied Jadanick.
"I am proud of you. You are one of a few
meant for greater things to come. I will not
stop you from doing that. I know why

Emma said something is wrong and that things are not the way they should be. Let's face it. I am not part of this. I know that I am in someone else's place and I am afraid that can get me killed," she paused and hugged Jadanick.

"I want you to keep me in your heart forever. When this is over come and find me. Promise Jay," said Sandra looking at Jadanick who sighed heavily and wiped a tear down his left cheek.

"I understand too. I wish I can make you one of us. I would have loved to see you for the rest of my life. But I understand. Even myself I know what you are talking about. When this is over, I will come and look for you OK? Look after yourself," said Jadanick lifting Sandra up. The two hugged for a very long time. They kissed. The others came when they heard the sobbing.

"What's going on. Are you guys okay?" asked Emma.

"I am leaving you. I am in the wrong place. But when this is over Jay we will be together again," said Sandra.

"Ah that's so sweet," replied Alina. For the first time Jadanick felt like himself. He felt like a burden had been lifted from his shoulders. He loved Sandra very much, but he knew it was better for her to go than for her to end up dead. Surely the magnificent warriors would only protect the Emperor and not even his wife unless she was pregnant with his son. Clearly if Sandra remained there. She would end up dead. That afternoon they had farewells. Sandra left, and no one knew where she went. Anywhere the world took her was okay as long as it was not at the Palace. That night the animals came back and growled all night outside. In the morning, the animals all had gone. They got into the car and drove off to the lake to see if the animals had left Shane's corpse back there.

"The animals freaked me last night. For the first time, they were growling outside, and they slept here as well," said Emma.

"That's very strange," replied Alina.

"I think I read something along those lines in one of the books at the library. In the book, they said the beginning of the end is marked by the spillage of the blood and the relentless growling and howling of the animals," explained Emma.

"You said the beginning of the end. What end?" asked Adonis.

"That marks the final ceremonial burial of the Emperor preparing him for the afterlife," Replied Jack.

"The Emperor has to be washed by the spilling of the blood of the enemy and be reunited with all the possession he had in this life," answered Emma.

"I took the diary from one of the cabinets. Does that mean that I have to return it afterwards?" asked Emma.

"Yes. Or else the animals will be after you," joked Jadanick. Everyone started laughing.

"You okay man?" asked Jack.

"Yes. I am okay. I just remembered when I was seven years old this is what I wanted to do. I have waited for eleven years for this. I am ready. It's time we do what we are meant to do. Let's find the Emperor's resting place and preserve his bloodline. I think I have the answers," Jadanick pointed at his tattoo. They all nodded in agreement.

"Has anyone had a copy of that map from Teekay?" asked Jack.

"I got one," replied Emma opening her handbag and taking out a folded paper and handing it to Jack.

"Per this map. The Emperor's resting place is the place where we dug that grave," said Jack.

"We know that but what we are saying is that he is not there. The question is where is he?" asked Emma. They arrived at the Lake but they couldn't find Shane's body or the animals. Jadanick since the day Sandra left he hadn't been himself. He started feeling down and started sleeping more than he normally did. They all knew it was because of the departure of Sandra. One night he woke up in the middle of the night. He was relentless and could not sleep. He went outside to smoke. He started thinking about the life he had as a musician. He remembered when he was shot at the age of seven and how that drove him to be one of the most successful musicians around. What am I doing here? I could be somewhere better right now. All this is just a dream. How many weeks now and we still can't find the Emperor? After all the Emperor is dead. That's not want I wanted to do with my life. My dream was to protect the highness the mighty Emperor. Not this what we are doing. I had plenty of money and a successful career. All this stopped making sense a long time ago. I think I must go back to my life. These were the thoughts that were coming to Jadanick's mind while he was smoking outside. In his mind, he was miles away thinking about all the bad things that had happened to him and how he still managed to stay alive. For the first time, he felt invincible. Death had knocked on his door several times but he refused to open the door. This time he knew that he had to look for his girlfriend Sandra and start rebuilding his life just like in the old days. There was nothing that was going to stand in his way. He made an oath that night to give all this just one last chance and he is out. Everyone was sleeping inside the main bedroom. No one had gone outside before at night since the days Teekay and Natasha were mauled to death. Jadanick realized that fear was his greatest enemy. He was in the middle of smoking his cigarette when he felt his hair standing up and a cold shiver going down his spine. He looked around and saw the whole crew surrounding animal. He could see the golden- shining eyes of the white lion looking at him with that kind of look that said move and you are dead. He stood there thinking. He wanted to scream at one point but when he remembered all the bad things that had happened to him he knew that the gods had chosen him for greater things. After all these animals, had not shown him any aggressive behavior. He knelt and touched the ground with one hand as if he was on the starting line of a marathon race. The animals started circling him. The big brown lion then joined the big white lion followed by the tiger and the rest of the animals. They all looked at him and waited for his move. In his head, he was that afraid that he did not know what to do. He did this because he remembered Sandra telling him that Jack did the same thing and the animals ran away. He was about to lie down with fear when the animals sat down too. He looked around and saw all the animals down surrounding him. He nearly froze to death with fear. He realized that the best thing is to remain still for some time. The animals posed no immediate danger. At that very moment he felt the most excruciating pain running down his spine. He looked upwards bending his back inwards. He growled in pain and the animals stood up and looked at him. He fainted there on the spot. The animals sat back on the ground and lay down as before and they slept surrounding Jadanick. He was shivering all night with cold. Early morning the animals woke up and left him sleeping there. In the morning, Alina woke up early and noticed that Jadanick was not in his bed. She didn't worry too much about it as he might have gone to the toilet or for a smoke. After sometime she started looking for Jadanick. She checked inside, but he was not there. She looked in the bathroom but he was not there. She decided to go outside that's when she saw him sleeping on the ground shivering. She called the others and Jack and Adonis carried him inside the palace. For days, he was in and out of unconsciousness.

"What's going on with Jadanick," asked Emma.

"We really do not know but it's like what you have experienced those days," replied Alina.

"Should we not lock him in one of the rooms?" asked Emma.

"Who locked you? Were you not free to walk? Do not be absurd why should we lock him in the room. Give us one good explanation why we should lock him," asked Adonis.

"He might be re-living someone else's past life. In the diary, they said that the former Emperor was found slumped to the ground after he entered the room with the magic stones. He was in a trance for days and when he woke up that's when the killing spree started. So, which part you didn't understand. Lock him in his own room until he is back," shouted Emma. They all looked at each other without knowing what to do.

"We are in this mess because no one did anything and you want us to go through the same too. No, no, no I am not going to sit and watch him destroy all of us. Jack help me move him to the next room," shouted Emma.

"That is not the way to handle this. You are overreacting," jibed Jack.

"You are not listening to me. Let's just put him in a separate room when he gets up and he is okay then we let him out," said Emma.

"Jack, are you going to help me or not?" asked Emma.

"No, I refuse because he is one of us. No one treated you like that. So, why should you do that to him? No. I am not part of this," shouted Jack who remained seated.

"Ok. Adonis give me a hand let us lift him up to the room next door," asked Emma. Adonis remained seated too.

"Adonis do not forget what happened to you," said Emma. Adonis looked at everyone and then got up. He complained about all this but he did help Emma.

"I am only helping you to put him in the room next door whether you lock him in there or not has nothing to do with me. Okay?" explained Adonis. They carried Jadanick to the room next door and Adonis left as fast as he can. Emma took the keys and locked the room. No one said anything they all just sat down.

"It's not right you know," said Jack looking at Emma who kept seated there without saying anything. They heard Jadanick growling next door and Emma forbade anyone to go there. They all slept. In the middle of the night the animals came back and started banging the door and making growling noises.

"Ewalinka! Eva! Open this door now?" shouted Jadanick. The rest of the group heard Jadanick banging the door shouting and screaming. They all came outside the door.

"Let him out. He is one of us for Christ's sake. Open the door Emma," shouted Jack. "We have to make sure that he is not going to harm us," responded Emma.

"Do not be silly why would I harm you. Open this door. If you do not want me here, just tell me I will go away you know," shouted Jadanick.

"Listen to me we have to make sure that he is okay," said Emma. Jadanick started banging the door shouting for the door to be opened.

"Listen. We will let him out I and Adonis we will talk to him for a while if he is acting strange in any way then we will put him back okay?" asked Jack.

"Ok. Trust me," said Jack. The door was opened and Jadanick got out.

"What do you think you are doing locking me inside? Do you know who I am? You do that again and you will be out of here," said Jadanick looking down. He did not look at anyone. He was about to go outside when Jack hold his hand.

"Hey, wait I need to talk to you for a minute," said Jack.

"Get your hands off me. Right now, I need to smoke," said Jadanick forcing his way outside. They all stood there and waited for him to come back.

"I told you, keep him locked until all the hallucinations had gone now look what you have done," said Emma taking back the door keys from Jack.

"You can't keep him locked in for a long time. He has gone just to smoke and he will be back," replied Jack with a bit of uneasiness. They waited for Jadanick but he did not return.

"Where is he now?" asked Emma. "Let's go and find him. He is not himself. Now you see why I locked in that room," said Emma. "It's partly your fault too you scared him away by locking him up," said Jack going outside to look for Jadanick. They all went outside and started calling his name.

"Jadanick!" shouted Alina.

"Jay, where are you?" shouted Emma.

"Jadanick where are you. Come back?" shouted Adonis. They looked all around but he was nowhere to be seen.

"What if the animals got him?" asked Alina.

"We have to go and find him," said Jack.

"Whoever is coming with me wear warm clothes and let's go," shouted Jack. They jumped in the car and drove off slowly looking for Jadanick. They went to every place they can think of but he was not there. They only returned to the palace to sleep when Alina suggested that maybe he took the opportunity to go and see Sandra. They all with no doubt agreed with that idea and they came back home and slept. Emma was fast asleep and suddenly she woke up to see Jadanick standing beside her bed looking at her. She took the bed cover and covered herself.

"What are you doing? Why are you standing there for?" shouted Emma. That woke Alina up as well as everyone else.

"What do you mean what am I doing? I just got back a few minutes ago," replied Jadanick going to sit on his bed.

"Welcome back Jadanick. We were starting to worry about you," said Adonis smiling at Jadanick.

"So, did you see her? You know? Did you have some TLC?" asked Adonis sitting next to Jadanick.

"See who?" asked Jadanick looking surprised.

"You know Sandra, your girlfriend," replied Adonis. They all looked at Jadanick waiting and expecting to hear him say yes. He looked even more confused, and he took off his jacket.

"I do not know what you are talking about?" replied Jadanick.

"What do you mean man, you know Sandra your girlfriend," said Adonis reminding Jadanick.

"Do you mean Sylvia? I did not go to see her. I went to the lake," replied Jadanick taking off his shirt it looked wet from afar.

"Who is Sylvia?" asked Emma.

"What do you mean gone to the lake?" asked Alina. He opened the clothes cabinet and took a warm t-shirt and wore it. They all looked at each other as he lay down on his bed and slept.

"Take his shirt let me see. Check if it's wet," asked Emma. Adonis got up and slowly tip toed toward Jadanick's bed. He knelt to pick up the t-shirt that was on the floor.

"What do you want," asked Jadanick. Adonis stood there for a while and looked at Emma, Alina and Jack.

"Pick-it up," asked Emma with a low voice. Adonis picked up the t-shirt by the tips of his fingers as it was very wet. He tips-toed backward.

"It's drenched, was in the lake for sure," replied Adonis. They all looked at each other and remained numb. Jadanick started going out at night and coming back in the morning to sleep. They started worrying about him. He spent less and less time with them. One night he was in the bathroom and he growled with pain and Alina tiptoed to see what was going on. Jadanick was standing in front of the bathroom mirror when Alina opened the door. He looked surprised and freighted as well. He looked at Alina with his eyes wide open. When Alina looked at him, his face was very scary his eyes had changed to match hers. He put his hand on her shoulder.

"Ewalinka, what do you want?" asked Jadanick.

"Let go of me Jay."
Jadanick let her go and he looked himself
in the mirror. His eyes had changed. He
smashed the mirror and staggered outside
the palace and disappeared.
"Jadanick is getting worse I do not think
he is himself," said Alina holding her
shoulder.
"What happened?" asked Emma.
"Something is really wrong. He can't even
remember me, today he called me
Ewalinka." Explained Alina.
"It's just a phase he will be okay soon,"
said Emma trying to comfort Alina.
"There is something more, even up to now
I can't tell what actually happened in
there," said Alina looking at Emma.
"What is it? You can tell me," asked
Emma.
"I heard him making these animal noises, I
went there to check, the door wasn't
closed. I slid it open just to see what was
going on with him. He grabbed my
shoulder and looked me into my eyes. I am
sure that his eyes matched mine," she
paused and looked at Emma.

"I swear why would I lie about something like that," asked Alina. There was a moment of silence.

"He is going through exactly what I went through," said Emma.

"Why his eyes matched mine. Am I in danger?" asked Alina afraid.

"No I do not think so. Sometimes his eyes match eyes of those in the vicinity as a warning. The ancient warriors used that gift. Or just because you went in there in secret. This was an asset, and a protection means centuries ago. You might have sacred him," replied Emma.

"Did you shout his name or knock the door first?" asked Emma.

"I can't remember but I do not think so," replied Alina.

"Call everyone we have to talk about this," asked Emma.

"Jack, Adonis come here please?" shouted Alina. The boys both came as soon as heard Alina shouting for them.

"Something happened this afternoon and I want everyone to know this. From today onward, do not go behind Jadanick. He is still reliving someone's past. He can easily lose it. Okay?" asked Emma. They all agreed and Alina explained what happened.

"Do not we think we should start following him. Where does he go every night? I think we should try to understand what he is going through," said Jack.

"I personally think that we should try to find out what happened in the last century so that we can at least anticipate what is going to happen to him," asked Emma.

"I do not think we should be worried about him. We should start to worry about ourselves now," said Adonis.

"Why did you say that Adonis? Jadanick is one of us," said Jack.

"Oh, sure he is one of us but he is no longer our friend I quote. He is making new friends now," said Adonis looking at the ladies with his eyes wide opened.

"What new friends?" asked Alina

"The animals," replied Adonis.

"Do not be silly. How is that possible?" asked Emma.

"You frightened him by locking him up

now he feels like the animals. I swear he is sleeping with them now. Every night he sleeps away from us he become closer to them than to us. Soon they will be synchronized. That's when we will be in danger," explained Adonis.

"You can't blame me for locking him up. I was trying to help him," shouted Emma.

"The more he is afraid of you the more he takes the animals side. Soon they will be together and I do not know what will happen after that," explained Jack.

"What can we do in this situation?"

"Go where ever he is sleeping and bring him back or sleep with him there too," said Adonis.

"I honestly cannot understand all this. Why is he sleeping outside with temperatures below freezing point? Is he mad? Is he trying to kill himself?" asked Alina.

"I bet he does not even feel the cold. His system is shutdown right now. He has no feelings whatsoever. He is like a person who has experienced trauma. He does not know pain. This is the kind of state he is in right now. I bet he is playing with the animals. He shows no fear so they do not attack him," said Adonis.

"So how long will this go on for?" asked Emma.

"It's anyone's guess. The great danger will come the day he will come out of this nightmare. We should try to anticipate that day. That day if he is with the animals and if he shows any fear. He is gone. The animals will maul him to death," added Adonis.

"We should try to find him, at least try to stop him from going back again," said Emma.

"Never stop him. I warn you. He leaves us because where ever he is going there are more benefits to him than what we are providing him with. Stopping him will make him see you as an enemy even if the benefits are temporary," replied Adonis.

"You do not want to upset him right now. He doesn't even know you, unless if you represent someone else in his small world," added Jack.

"Are you sure he is not going to see Sandra

and doing all this stuff as a cover-up?" asked Emma.

"Honestly I do not think he even remembers who Sandra is. He mentioned a one Sylvia the other day," explained Jack.

"So, all you guys you blame me for locking him up?" asked Emma feeling guilty.

"Listen, this was going to happen, anyway. He had been through a lot in his life. I think he is very strong but all this might have shaken his faith and trust. Sandra's departure is what triggered this more than anything else. Some people can go through tough times easily but one day all this can come back to haunt when you least expected," explained Adonis.

That night Emma woke up in the middle of the night grabbed the car keys and drove off. She drove for some time looking everywhere for Jadanick but with no luck. She decided to drive to the lake. On her way, a lot of questions were running through her head. The feelings of guilty somehow gave her courage. She started fearing for Jadanick's life. If he is not himself, then maybe the animals might turn against him and kill him. She switched off the car lights as she approached the lake and drove slowly. She parked the car and waited further away from the lake. She waited there thinking about all this. She was about to start the car engine and drive off when she heard something jumping in the lake water. She looked and saw the animals. She waited there for some time not knowing what to do. She switched the car engine on and drove very slowly toward the lake after making sure that all the doors were locked. She came close to the lake and stopped the car. Her heart was beating very fast. All the animals were there but Jadanick was not there. Two minutes later he resurfaced and laughed. She was shocked to see him. He pushed his hair backwards removing the water. He swam toward the lake shore. He was nude and temperatures were below freezing point. He got out and walked toward the animals.

"No! Jadanick,, she shouted in the car as a reflex before touching her mouth. Jadanick acted as if he heard that and stopped and looked in the direction she was. She nearly got out of the car and ran to him. To her surprise, he walked between the animals touching them before going to sit naked among them. It felt like a dream. He started touching the tiger before the animal jumped into the lake. He knelt and touched all one by one. Each one he touched then jumped into the lake. The animals swung for a while and then went out of the lake waters. When the weather was getting very cold, he got up and jumped back into the lake again. Emma started the car engine and drove away from the lake. She headed home to the palace and slept in Alina's bed, hugged her tight and slept.

CHAPTER THIRTEEN

Early morning Jadanick came back and looked at Emma's bed but she was not there. He looked at Jack's bed and saw Jack sleeping. He looked at Adonis' bed and saw Adonis sleeping when he looked at Alina's bed he saw both the ladies sleeping. He went to the bathroom. He was there for some time. He looked in the mirror and saw that his eyes' color had changed to match Emma's. He felt that excruciating pain he felt before the day he started sleeping outside. The pain was unbearable that he slumped to the floor. He let out the loudest growling sound they have ever heard sending everyone into a panic. The all woke up very frightened. Emma started crying holding onto Alina. Adonis and Jack woke up and ran to his rescue. They entered the unlocked bathroom and found Jadanick on the floor. He opened his eyes and looked at them. He had matched Emma's eye color. As soon as Jack touched him he his eyes changed and matched Jack's eyes. Adonis was about to touch him when Jack shouted.

"Do not touch him. Lift him let's put him in his bed." They lifted him up and as they entered the bedroom where all of them slept Emma fainted with fear. Jack looked at Emma, Alina and then Adonis before he nodded his head and pointed to the next room with his head. They took Jadanick and laid him on the bed next door. He was going in and out of unconsciousness. They came out quickly and locked the door. They ran back to the bedroom and helped Emma.

"Damn! What is going on? What happened to Jadanick? It's worse than I thought," said Adonis.

"I do not know what to say. I didn't think

it will be this bad," said Jack putting his hands on his face.

"What happened to Emma?" asked Adonis.

"Fear. She seemed to be re-living someone else's past and these two they have a history between them," replied Jack .

"I was reading the diary it seemed centuries ago. The person Jadanick is reliving was the Emperor. Somehow, he found a way of taking the powers from them and threatened to kill them. Whether he succeeds or not, no one knows," replied Alina.

"Did you see the color of his eyes? They changed when I touched him to match mine," said Jack.

"Damn! That freaked me out?" said Adonis.

"That's how he can identify the person in his vicinity and whether an enemy or not," said Jack.

"Maybe we should put Emma in the room with the magic stones for her to recover quickly," suggested Adonis.

"If that helps I do not see why not," replied Jack.

"No I do not think it's a good idea. Per the diary, they only put someone in the room with the magic stones as a way of calling for help or if there was an enemy," said Alina.

"But also, if someone is not feeling well as in this case, right?" asked Adonis.

"Right... but," said Alina.

"Hm. No buts," said Adonis before he carried Emma to the room with the magic stones. As soon as Emma was in this room, the stones started to release the smoke. The green stones started to glow giving the room a green color. They made sure that Jadanick's door was locked and that the door to the room with the magic stones was closed. In the bedroom, there was Alina, Adonis and Jack talking.

"All this is taking a nasty turn. If we have powers to protect the Emperor why is everything so difficult?" asked Adonis.

"I think this is just a phase soon to pass," said Jack.

"You think so?" asked Alina.

"I know so hang in there soon we will wake up and find out that all this was just a dream," replied Jack.

"Thanks. But I still know that you are just saying this so that I do not worry too much. Right?" said Alina.

"No. I really mean it," said Jack. Alina got up and opened her arms asking Jack for a hug.

"Ah, you know what to say. That's exactly what I wanted to hear," said Alina. The two hugged each other for a while before Adonis got up.

"I am just going to check on Emma and Jay," he left and closed the door behind him. The two, Alina and Jack were away in another world for a while talking about other things than the current problems.

"It's funny we never heard the chance to talk just you and me. For the past week's, it has been the talk about searching the Emperor and all that stuff," said Jack.

"At least I am glad we finally had the chance," replied Alina.

"We will all be okay. Soon we will find the bloodline of the Emperor. I can feel that," said Jack.

"Are you not just saying that just to please

me? I think I have seen that look in your eyes before," said Alina.

"What look? You mean this look?" asked Jack making a funny face-look. Alina couldn't stop laughing and somehow Alina opened her eyes to see Jack's eyes in very proximity. Before she had a chance to say something Jack had already planted a smacker on her lips. She stood up angrily and confused yelling and shouting.

"No Jack! We cannot do that. I do not mean it that way. I should remain pure and true to the Emperor. Are you stupid? Are you trying to get yourself killed? We should be worrying about Emma and Jadanick and not you getting some ideas." Alina had a point. They were to remain true and pure to the Emperor.

"You know what? I think you are right. Let's go and check up on them right now," said Jack getting up.

"Ok. Jack lets go," replied Alina.

"I am very sorry. I just got carried away," said Jack.

"Apology accepted," replied Alina.

"OMG! What happened here? Where is

Adonis? What's all this?" Screamed Alina standing in a pool of blood. The door to the room where Emma was sleeping was wide opened. They stood there for a few seconds looking at the trail of blood going toward the door. They quickly rushed inside the room where Emma was sleeping. She was there sleeping on the bed. Quickly Jack flipped the bed sheets and touched on the bed and Emma checking for blood.

"She is okay!" shouted Jack.

"Adonis! Adonis! Come let's check Jadanick's room," said Jack going outside the room with the magic stones. Alina followed him. He tried to open the door, but the door was locked from outside.

"Where is the key?" asked Jack.

"I do not know Adonis had the key," replied Alina. They looked through the window Jadanick was their sleeping and the door was locked from the outside.

"I guess Jadanick is okay. I think it's the animals again. They took Adonis. Listen! Let's get Emma out of the room with the magic stones and into the bedroom. Lock the door from the inside until I come back.

Do not come outside until I come back. Okay?" asked Jack holding Alina's shoulders.

"Okay," replied Alina getting into the bedroom and locking the door behind her. Jack remember the day the animals dragged Natasha away. They had delayed following the animals, and that did cost Natasha her life. This time quickly he jumped into the car and drove like he had never driven before. Only he can save Adonis' life. He remembered the last time something like this happened. The animals had no intention of killing Natasha. It was an accident. The way they carried her was the same way they carry their young ones. The intention was not to kill. It was different to what happened to Teekay. Teekay was mauled with intent and he died on the spot I think in minutes. Jack was hoping that the blood was from a leg or something not life threatening. He knew the animals were on their side. He was still thinking and re-living the day he chased after the animals here too trying to save Natasha when he saw the lake in front of him. He stopped for a while and thought why Adonis did not warn them of the danger surely, he knew there was a danger because his watch would have given him the option to subjugate. He was about to get out of the car when the tiger gnawed at him showing him its teeth. He quickly jumped back into the car and urged forward. He drove to near the lake shore. The other animals had surrounded Adonis. He looked at Adonis who looked dead. He did not move for a while. Suddenly he raised his arm and two of the animals got up and instantly mauled him. They then went to sit down with the rest of the animals. Jack was seeing all this. He opened the car door and slowly got out. He looked for something from the car but then again decided to walk toward the animals hoping to lie down. As soon as the animals had sensed him they all rose and ran after him. He stood there planning to lie down on the ground but the animals did not stop coming. Quickly he ran back into the car nearly being dragged out by the tiger that banged on the door hurting itself that it started to bleed. Adonis was still alive but bleeding to death. Jack had to do something. Time was running out. Adonis' life was at risk. Jack had never felt so helpless. He had assumed that the animals would run away as they did the first time in Natasha's case. But to his surprise they had become more ferocious. Jack quickly pressed the horn as long and loud as he can. He thought of running down the animals with the car. He was about to drive forward when Adonis reacted but that was a mistake. The animals sprinted toward him and most of them did bite him and kept holding onto him. They released the bite, and he moved again a bit probably giving up his last breath and this angered the white lion that it jumped on him inserting its paws-nails into his chest and biting his neck never letting go. Jack jumped in his seat banging his head on the roof of the car. He felt like he died himself it was the most gruesome thing he had ever seen. He felt sad and helpless. He looked in the lake further down, looking for the position of his spaceship. He had never felt this kind of fear and helplessness before. The act of the white lion did send out strong signs of intent. Is this what protecting the Emperor really meant? For some time, he just sat there. The white lion had hinted to him what was to happen. To serve the Emperor also meant to die a gruesome death. Everything made sense. He remembered the first days he arrived here, the lake was the only place that kept coming to his mind. He had made this pilgrimage journey to this lake for several times now. He had lost count of how many times he had been here. As he was thinking about all this something even worse happened. The animals stood up and all formed a circled around him and sat around him as they had done to the car that they were in the other day. Jack nearly wet his pants with fear even worse when he saw what the animals did next. They stood up after sometime all seven of them and circled him again and this time all of them carried him and all went into the lake water carrying him. They swam toward the place he had landed and circled again in the water and laid him to rest in the water. They all started growling and circling the place. After that they all got out of the water and ran away from that place heading in the direction of the palace. The first idea that came to Jack's mind was to run as fast as he can away from all this. He wanted just to jump into the lack waters, into his spaceship and away from there.

"Is this the meaning of, to protect, to serve and to honor the Emperor?"

Jack asked himself. He sat there thinking. He remembered that the animals had dug up Shane from the grave and brought him here. Shane himself had died here in the lake. Natasha was thrown into the lack. Jack quickly opened the grove compartment of the car and looked for the diary. He flipped through the diary and came to the page with a quotation;

Just before the end there shall be a period of cleansing which initiates the beginning of the end which shall be marked by the spillage of blood on the surface of the land where the Emperor shall be buried and where all his possessions shall be placed in the earth to prepare him for afterlife. Jack quickly took out the copy of Jadanick's tattoo made by Teekay before he died. He looked at it. Surely the Emperor's burial place should be in the palace. So why the animals are killing and throwing the Emperor's warriors in the lake instead of the grave at the palace. Does that mean that the Emperor drowned in the lake? Jack could not find answers to this. He remembered Alina. She had somehow got out of his mind. She was a very strong willed lady. She was very beautiful and very intelligent too. At one point, he had forgotten his mission. Quickly he started the car engine and drove home to the palace. He looked at his watch but there was no any message, so he assumed Alina was okay otherwise she would have sent him a call for help. He drove back home to the palace with his heart heavy with what he had seen and the whole meaning of his mission. He arrived home only to be greeted by the angry animals. He parked the car at the entrance and jumped straight into the palace building. He went inside. The animals had tried to enter the building. The door outside was stretched heavily.

"Alina! Alina! It is Jack opened the door!" shouted Jack. Quickly the door opened. "What happened?" asked Jack. Her eyes were swollen. She had been crying heavily. "Are you okay what happened?" asked again Jack.

"We are all going to die. The animals surely, they wanted to come in and take us all. None stop they kept banging and stretching the door. I tried to send you a call for help but," Alina didn't finish talking before she sobbed heavily.

"You said you will come back soon, but you had been gone forever. I never thought to see you again. I thought something happened to you too," said Alina sobbing. Jack realized that he spent a lot of time daydreaming at the lake. He apologized and asked her a question.

"So why you didn't send me a message or a call for help?" asked Jack.

"Because Emma is in a trance. She is

jamming all the signals. She was in the room with the magic stones. It's like a call for help. No wonder why the animals are relentless," quipped Alina. Jack stood up and walked up and down for a while.

"I think we are safer in here and we should remain inside. I think the animals will go away in the morning. If you want, we all go away from this palace. I promise you that I will do anything to keep all of us safe. For now, I will go and check Jadanick. Ok I will be back soon," said Jack standing up and going to the next room. He didn't wait for Alina to reply. He checked through the window and saw Jadanick seated. He quickly raised his head and looked at Jack.

"Are you okay?"asked Jack but Jadanick did not reply he just kept looking at him turning his head left and right. Suddenly Jack did not see what happened but Jadanick seemed to have jumped from where he was seated to the bars on the window in a flash. Jack jumped backward and fell to the ground. He lay on the floor and looked at Jadanick through the window. He licked the window with his tongue and went to seat down. The morning arrived and Jack woke up. He walked to the door, and he opened the door slowly to check if the animals were still there before he felt the paw-nails of one of the animals running down his thigh. He quickly closed the door and went back into the house.

"Alina I need your help!" Shouted Jack. Alina came running, and she stood there for a while in disbelief. Quickly she knelt to bandage his thigh.

"What happened did you go outside?" asked Alina shocked by all this.

"No I just opened the door and one of the animals was waiting to pounce on me," replied Jack.

"Are you telling me that the animals are still there?" asked Alina. When Jack looked at Alina for the first time she saw fear in his eyes. She saw death. Death was written all over his face. He had changed in a day. He looked lifeless. His eyes gave away. He had no hope at all. He looked like a person waiting to die. Alina could read everything.

"What did you see at the lake?" asked Alina. Jack did not reply straight away. He squinted his eyes in pain.

"What did you see at the lake?" repeated Alina.

"Adonis being mauled to death. I am sorry I couldn't do anything. I was so scared. It was brutal. He called for help, but I just sat there hopeless until his last breath. Even after he had died, they hold on to him. It was gruesome to watch," sobbed Jack.

"We are all going to die, right?" asked Alina. Jack did not reply he looked at this thigh and tried getting up. He limped into the bedroom where Emma was sleeping like a baby, peaceful as if there is no tomorrow. Jack went to the window and looked outside. He saw the animals still there sat outside waiting for them.

"Check on Jadanick but do not talk to him," suggested Jack.

"Ok," replied Alina.

She looked through the window. She saw Jadanick standing facing outside. Jadanick was looking outside through the window.

Alina was about to go back into the bedroom where everyone else was when Jadanick started banging the door asking Alina to open the door. Hysterically like a hungry lion he punched the door shouting and screaming.

"Open the door now! Open the door! Alina open this door now! OMG! No. Please open the door. I beg you open the door! Jack! Jack! Come here now! Please open the door Jack! Jack Alina! open this door now!"

He banged the door so hard and shook it that the rest of the room shook too. In the commotion, Emma woke up.

"Jack what should I do!? Can I open the door? Jack answer me now?" shouted Alina.

"No! Do not open the door!" said Jack sitting down on the bed.

Alina ran to the bedroom and pushed the door open. It all happened like in slow motion. Alina slowly pushing the door and facing Jack who was more concerned about his leg than anything else. He had assumed that Jadanick was hallucinating. Alina looked away from Jack and saw

Emma. She had opened the curtained, and she was looking through the window. As Alina entered the room, she in slow motion, looked at her and shouted something with her eyes wide opened. Her face said it all; death. She pointed at the window shouting something. She quickly, but still in slow motion looked again outside the window. Soon she quickly covered her mouth and instantly covered her eyes. Jack looked at Alina and saw the look on her face which also said it all, death. He jumped onto the window panel and looked outside. In slow motion, he screamed shaking his head in disbelief. For that moment, he didn't feel any pain in his thigh leg. He made his way outside the room as fast as he can. All this time they could not hear each other because of the noise that was coming from the next room. Jadanick was shouting like he had never done before. Shaking the walls, trying to break the door and the window to no avail. They all looked outside and saw Jack running and limping outside as well as he ran toward the yard of the palace. Still in slow motion, he fell to the ground and quickly got up. He threw something he had in his hand at the animals. For a while the animals stopped and looked at Jack. In slow motion, they quickly grabbed what looked like a lady by the thigh leg and dragged her with them. Jack followed them for a while before falling to the ground. He rolled over on the ground and got up he limped back to the car and quickly turned the car around and drove off. Jadanick cried like a baby. Alina ran and hugged Emma the two threw themselves on the bed and cried inconsolably.

CHAPTER FOURTEEN

Jack followed the animals he drove as fast as he can be given the circumstances that he had his thigh injured. He arrived as soon as the animals arrived. He got out of his car and quickly limped toward the animals. He could see Sandra lying there surrounded by the animals. He had no fear at all. He limped very close to the animals. He waited a moment and took a long breath. He sat down first for a few minutes tightening the bandage as his wound had started bleeding. He got up and walked toward the animals near the lake. He had a flashback of how Adonis died. He had been a coward, he had just seated inside the car instead of helping him. Even worse this time. He had made a judgmental error that resulted in Sandra being mauled on the thigh. Even if he survived the animals, he knew for sure that Jadanick was going to kill him, anyway. He chose to die like a magnificent warrior and to save others the anguish. He remembered all these years he had waited to protect the Emperor. For some reason, he stopped and realized that the Emperor was in the Lake. Damn! He felt like a fool. All these months the animals tried to point them in the right direction but they were too busy to notice. He remembered talking to Adonis. Adonis had suggested that the Emperor was in the lake. The grave they had dug was his original place of burial but the weather had changed everything. Him being without a successor the Chief priest send a priest to help preserve the Emperor's DNA so that future warriors will be able to track his bloodline through DNA. The sudden temperature changes from warm to hot days to extremely cold nights had meant the destruction of the Emperor's DNA. If they came here to preserve his DNA why must they die. It didn't make any sense. Jack arrived a few feet from the animals and stood there tired rather than afraid. The white lion stood up and growled and started walking toward Jack. Jack was about to lie down and play dead when Sandra lifted her head to look at him. Jack remembered how Adonis died. He had resisted death, and the animals kept mauling him. He felt sorry for Sandra. He shouted to alert and divert attention to him. All the animals got up and followed the white lion toward Jack.

"To serve, to protect and to honor the Emperor for eternity."

Jack pledged his allegiance to the Emperor and prepared for death. Sandra lifted her head again and looked at Jack as the animals approached him. He closed his eyes. He realized that it was going to be either him or her. He knew the animals preferred him. They had just used Sandra as a bet to trap him. They had tried this trick before with Natasha but the plan did not go per plan.

"What kind of animals are these? The Emperors."

He asked himself and answered himself as well before smiling. These were clever animals they had underestimated them. If he had listened in the first place they could have the Emperor's bones and extracted his DNA and managed to find his bloodline by now. But they had wasted the opportunity they had. Now probably it was now too late to preserve his DNA. The only option now was for the animals to reunite with the Emperor and all his possessions including them too. He stood there thinking that this somehow was cruelty to some extent. They had a chance to quickly find the Emperor, get his DNA and search for his bloodline but unfortunately, they all must be reunited with the Emperor. The only thing that did not make sense was that this Emperor was not their Emperor. Where was their Emperor? The animals came into attacking distance. He closed his eyes preparing for the worst. He remembered reading somewhere that you cannot fight the Emperor's warriors. So, no matter hard that might sound he stood there and prepared for death.

"Ah," Jack screamed in pain.

The white lion had inserted its teeth in his calf muscle before dragging him to the lake. The others didn't attack as he had expected. He was dragged to the lake and left next to Sandra. He looked at her. She was okay. He sighed with relief that she was not badly hurt. She just had puncture wounds. He remembered the wound on Natasha's thigh that was horrific. He also realized that probably Natasha fought back whereas Sandra went with the floor.

"I remembered you playing dead," whispered Sandra. Jack realized that there were big chances that Sandra can survive. "When I go with the animals to the other side. You quickly get up and run to the car and run okay?" whispered Jack. Sandra nodded fearing to be torn apart. Jack got up, and the animals got up too. He limped to the other side before the lion inserted its teeth again this time in the already wounded thigh. He let out the loudest noise. This was a wake up call for Sandra. She got up and ran to the car without even looking back. She got into the car and started driving the car toward the animals. This really aggravated the animals. The tiger inserted its teeth in his shoulder and the other lion inserted its teeth in his other calf.

"No! Go! Run!" shouted Jack. She stopped the car and looked at Jack, she sobbed uncontrollably and started reversing. When the animals have seen, the car going away they let go of him. She drove back to the palace. The animals stood up and circled Jack and then sat down circling him. He realized that it was just a matter of time before he is mauled to death. He felt the most excruciating pain coming from his bite wounds. He looked back at his life. He realized that he was one of the few destined for glory. He prepared to die with honor. The other two animals got up and started running following the car. The circle was not completed. Jack remembered reading a passage about the one who shall unite all the one with the power to see in this world and the world of the gods. He remembered seeing the cougar seating last to complete the chain. He looked around and the cougar and the brown lion were missing. He felt very hopeful. Animals were not very fast in the water, in fact most were afraid of the water. He slowly put his hand in his pocket. He felt the key to the spaceship. To hell with all this I am going home. He said to himself. He calculated how many splashes he had to make toward his ship. He planned to jump into the water and act as if he had drowned at least the animals won't follow him and to swim under water as fast as he can toward the ship. He had a big chance. He looked up to the sky and smiled. He was about to jump into the water when suddenly, the white lion inserted its teeth in his thigh muscles and never to release him. The other animals returned. He didn't even bother to look until when he heard Alina's voice. He felt his world plunging down. He felt like he had died. This was the worst scenario. At this moment, he felt helpless he felt it was better to die. The white lion did not release him after he tried to escape. He had started to lose blood.

"Jack!" shouted Alina.

"Can you swim? Crawl toward me do not worry if you are coming toward the lake they won't attack you. She crawled toward Jack. Put your hand in my pocket quickly. Take the key to my spaceship it is just a few meters from here. When I fight, and struggle with these animals you jump into the water. Swim underneath and press the button as soon as you enter the water. By the time, you reach the spaceship it should all be together and insert the key in the grove and fly home. Okay," said Jack. Alina did not reply she just sobbed.

"Hang in there and do what I said okay?" asked Jack shouting, and this earned him plenty of teeth in his other thigh. The pain just made him wriggle as hard as he can. All the animals came in force and inserted their teeth into Jack's body. Alina just flipped into the water. She pressed the key to the ship. She swam her best and by the time she reached the ship. The two piece of the ship had already joined together, she inserted the key and slowly the ship lifted above the water and the door opened. She jumped into the ship and the door was about to close when she felt her jacket being pulled toward the lake waters. Quickly she removed the jacket and closed the ship door. She activated auto pilot inserted the coordinates, and the ship rose from above the lake. She looked down and saw Jack surrounded by the animals. She stood still and saluted him. The ship rose and left. The white lion jumped on Jack and inserted into paw-nails into his chest and bite him in the neck. Soon after the animals circled around him and took him inside the lake waters. They buried him under water in the lake. They got out and quickly made their way toward the palace. Jadanick when he saw the love of his life being dragged away by the animals he knew that she was dead. He remembered what happened to Natasha. He cried inconsolably.

"You better let the animals eat you too. If you come back, I am going to kill you

myself," shouted Jadanick. He blamed
Jack for locking him up, He blamed Emma
for starting that in the first place. He cried
like a baby with saliva and tears drooling
down. He loved Sandra very much. He
didn't understand why she came back
ignoring him. He had clearly asked her not
to return but to wait for him. Why then
did she come back? Why these Moran's did
not open the door when he asked them to.
Surely that infuriated him. He punched
the walls until all his hands were swollen
up. He broke the windows with his fist. All
these years whenever bad things happened
to him he had never reacted he kept
putting everything in his jar. This time the
jar was full, and it had just exploded. He
felt enormous energy. That he punched the
door sending the whole room shaking. He
looked in the mirror which was in the
room he was in. He saw Emma. He looked
again in the mirror in disbelieve his eyes
had turned blue. He punched the walls and
stood there. He remembered how he first
met Sandra. She had been there for him
through thick and thin. He felt that he

loved her very much. He kept asking himself why she had come back. Why she had ignored him for the first time. This was out of character. He looked in the mirror again and saw his eyes still blue. For some reasons, he thought about Sandra. He looked down the sink and saw blood coming from his hands. He opened the sink tape water. And pushed the broken mirror glasses into the sink basin. He looked again in the mirror. His eyes color had changed to match that of Sandra's. He closed his eyes, and he looked again in the mirror this time his eye color had matched that of Emma's. Suddenly he heard someone behind him.

"Jay," said Sandra softly touching Jadanick. He felt being afraid of being locked in and he feared Emma he didn't look to see who it was in his mind he knew it was Emma. He just looked in the sink basin and took a broken glass, turned around and embedded the glass in her neck.

"OMG! Emma. I mean Sandra! OMG! What have I done! OMG! OMG!" screamed

Jadanick louder than he had done in the first place. He thought Sandra was dead after being dragged away by the animals. She was still alive. He cried and cried until he looked in the mirror again and saw his eye color change to a dark blue color. He was about to leave the room he was in when Emma suddenly appeared. She looked on the floor and saw a lot of blood and Sandra laying down dead. Jadanick was still holding the broken mirror in his hand with blood dripping from it. She remembered being afraid of him. The main reason she locked him up in that room. Also, the main thing which has set up a chain of events leading to the death of Sandra. Jadanick remembered that it was her who came to the lake and saw him playing with the animals that night. Jadanick realized that Emma had manipulated Sandra in coming back, most likely in false pretends, as to help make him get back to normal again after he lapsed. All this was in false presence he knew it. She had a bad motive. He looked at his dead girlfriend and remembered

Emma accusing him of trying to kill her. He was holding the broken mirror when she entered the room. He tried to explain that it was an accidental. Without thinking he shouted.

"It was an accident I thought it was you," he quickly realized what he had just said and before he knew it Emma turned around and started running away. Quickly he holds her dress. She wriggled to escape, but he hugged her from behind with his left hand putting his hand just on her chin and with the right hand he pushed the broken mirror into her throat.

"Emma! Emma! Jadanick! Jadanick lets go," he heard Alina calling he quickly looked throughout the window and saw a spaceship. He knelt and touched Sandra. "You know that I love you. I wish I can trade places with you right now. It was an accident. I swear. I had thought that you were dead. Forgive me Darling. Please forgive me. You are my heart. See you in afterlife." Jadanick kissed her on the lips and sobbed like a baby before getting up. He lifted her up and put her on the bed. He went just outside the room. He knelt beside Emma. He sobbed again uncontrollably.

"It hurts when you do not believe me. See what happened? You believed stupid things. You should have trusted me. I was one of you. Now see what happened. Your wish somehow fulfilled."

He leaned down and kissed her his tears dropping down on her face. He lifted her up and walked into the room where Sandra lay dead on the bed. He put them together and sat down. He cried for a while. He stood up on the side of the bed and saluted.

"To serve, to protect and to honor for eternity." He covered them with a bad spread and left the palace heading to the spaceship. Alina was glad to see Jadanick. She shouted again.

"Emma! Emma! Come on let's go we do not have time," hysterically shouted Alina.

"Jadanick why did you not tell Emma. She is taking too long," Jadanick looked backward and saw a car coming from the other side.

"Emma left as soon as you left. I guess she

is dead too," explained Jadanick.

"Damn it! I told her to stay and wait for me! Let's go and find her," said Alina feeling sad. She was very lucky to be alive. Jack had saved her life. He died with honor a true magnificent bodyguard.

"Why you didn't ask for Sandra? Why you only asked for Emma?" asked Jadanick. Alina was miles away. She was looking downward hoping to see Emma. She tried to search and link with her but for some reason all signals were jammed and that can only happen when she is in the palace and in the room with the magic stones or near it.

"Why you do not answer me?" asked Jadanick.

"You were saying?" asked Alina.

"I was asking you why you did not shout for Sandra as well, you only shouted for Emma and myself?" asked Jadanick. Alina looked lost for some time before she replied.

"I do not know what you are talking about, as far as I know Sandra died. I saw her being dragged away by the animals in front of everyone. Did you not see that?" asked Alina. Jadanick did not reply. He looked even more confused. So, she knew she was dead but what happened? How did she get back? These were the questions that were rushing in and out of Jadanick's head. He felt very sad. He wished he had saved Emma, but he felt betrayed too. He wished he can sleep for a while. His head was heavy and about to explode with thoughts, guilty feelings and the feelings of being betrayed. At one point, he felt that maybe he was hallucinating all this time. Alina tried again searching for Emma's signal but all the signals were jammed. Damn what was going on. Something was wrong. Alina looked at Jadanick. He was fast asleep. She saw an opportunity and took it. She turned back the spaceship to the palace. She landed the ship and got out quickly without thinking. She ran back to the palace and was about to enter the palace. She stopped for a while. She looked and saw a car she had never seen before parked outside. Fear struck her, but she had no time to waste she walked slowly and very carefully toward the palace entrance. She entered the building. She went straight to the room with the magic stones.

"Emma! Emma!", she shouted, but no one answered Emma was not in there. She left and entered the main bedroom where they all slept. She shouted Emma's name again but there was no answer. She was about to go out when she heard some coughing from the room next door where Jadanick was locked in. She peeped through the window but could not see anyone. She was a few feet away when she heard someone coughing again. She came back and opened the door and entered the room. There was someone on the bed after all. She walked slowly the bed and quickly flipped the bedsheets.

"Emma! toward Sandra?", she freaked out. She touched them both. Emma was still alive. Sandra was still alive too, but she had lost a lot of blood. Sandra after being stabbed using Shane's watch had subjugated to Emma and Emma somehow, she had managed to subjugate to someone's else just before Jadanick struck. The victim was the guy who had just arrived. He had accepted subjugating the very first time he arrived. Emma did not say anything her eye color was the same as Jadanick's. Alina checked Emma's eyes. She knew who had slashed Emma's throat. "Jadanick," she whispered. Emma opened her eyes and looked at Alina.

"What happened to Sandra? I thought she was dead?" asked Alina.

"That's what I thought too but then she turned up with only puncture holes. Full of life she explained what had happened. That Jack had saved her life. I spoke to her for some time before I agreed her to see Jadanick. I think that's when it happened."

"Who did you subjugate to? Was it Jadanick?" asked Alina.

"Why you ask? Is he dead, Jadanick? Where is he?" asked Emma.

"It was to someone... eh. the Priest," said Emma opening her eyes and pointing at Alina.

"The Priest? Who is the Priest?" asked

Alina.

"I do not know. How am I supposed to know that?" asked Emma.

"I think I know who the Priest is. I have seen a car parked outside. It could be him. So, I guess you killed him," said Alina looking at Emma. A cold shiver of fear ran through Emma's spine.

"Jadanick was not himself when he tried to kill you. He has come back now, and he is remorseful. I put him in the spaceship and we are all going home in the same spaceship as him. Okay?" said Alina.

"Are you crazy? That monster slashed me. Look he slashed his own girlfriend. What kind of person would do that? He is an animal. I am not going in the same spaceship as him. You give me back my watch I kill him now."

"Emma, we are going home. You want to stay here or you want to go home?" asked Alina.

"Do I have an option? I guess let's go home. But as soon as I arrive I am going to the president and tell him that that monster cut me like he is cutting a bunny," said Emma.

"I will confess too that you tried to set him up by your silly mistrust and accusations. I will also confess that you have alone locked him up. That in its own, set up a chain of events leading to his breakdown and a chain of events that followed. I will also provide a signed written statement that despite his disagreement you went and invited his girlfriend back on false pretends. Pretending to try to help him but knowingly that he was in a bad state and therefore fragile. Can I go on and on?" asked Alina.

"All right. I guess let's just go home," quipped Emma.

"Ok wait here I will be back soon. I will take Sandra first okay," said Alina taking Sandra to the spaceship. Alina lifted Sandra and carried her to the spaceship. She opened her eyes and Alina smiled. Alina arrived at the ship. She saw Jadanick fast asleep and Alina looked at Sandra and pointed at Jadanick and winked an eye. Alina walked to the car that was parked outside. She opened the door. She saw a man on the driver's seat with his throat slashed. Quickly he opened his eyes and hold Alina on her throat.

"Why are you trying to kill me? I protect the Emperor. I am holy and no man or woman shall touch me I am the temple priest from the Shaolin priest. Who are you? Identify yourself. Or you die right now," shouted the Priest.

"Has the Emperor been found? Why we need a priest?" asked Alina not concerned about the threat of death.

"Jay my love. Jay," said Sandra touching Jadanick waking him up. Jadanick had slept since taking off and as far as he knew he was back home. He just wiped his eyes without looking at the person who had touched him.

"Have we arrived home," asked Jadanick. He looked in the ship's mirror and saw that his eye color had changed and that it had matched Sandra's, very light blue. He looked again in the tiny mirror and felt like crying.

"I love you Sandra I am very sorry," said Jadanick feeling guilty that he had killed his own girlfriend.

"Do not be sorry I still love you. I know you didn't mean it," said Sandra leaning forward. Jadanick jumped forward and banged his head on the upper dashboard of the spaceship.

"Alina! I mean Sandra. I thought…", Jadanick just couldn't believe it. He pinched himself and kissed her. They both cried together. He felt more pain every time he looked at her. He just realized that whatever he was going to do for the rest of his life, he will always be haunted by this day. He realized it will be an unbearable thing to do. That scare signaled the end of their love. He was very happy. The scars will always be there and he was afraid that one day he might start feeling like the Emperor. He realized what he had to do. He took his tongue and put it all in Sandra's mouth.

"Now you want to kill me with your tongue. Ha?" asked Sandra pausing for a while.

"You want to choke me to death Ha. Jadanick?" remarked Sandra.

"No Darling. Every time you look in the mirror and see the scar just feel my tongue in your mouth. And if anyone asks just say my boyfriend has a sharp tongue and he can't see properly."
"Now I understand why they used to call you. The Unpredictable. I love you Jay, always,", said Sandra.
They both laughed and hugged.

CHAPTER FIFTEEN

It was the fighting that was going on the ground that changed everything. Jadanick realized that he will never see Sandra again. They had talked about this the first days. The end had surely begun. The magnificent warriors had to fight the priest. This was part of the ceremony to prepare the afterlife of the Emperor. In situations where an Emperor has no heir to the throne and no magnificent warriors. The priest before he dies he must kill or get the Emperor killed. The priest should know the resting place of the Emperor so that he will pass the message to the future priest where to find the Emperor's DNA and assign a new Emperor from his bloodline. The magnificent warriors must revenge the Emperor's death by killing the priest and this paves the way for his afterlife. The priests betrayed the Emperor by getting him killed so the magnificent warriors must revenge his death. Jadanick knew what was need of him. He reprogrammed the spaceship and entered new coordinates. He looked at Sandra.

"I love you very much. If I had to redo this again. I will choose you in this life and in after life."

He kissed her.

"Sandra, thank you for coming into my life," he didn't even wait to hear her say something. He jumped out of the ship. Closed the door and locked it from outside. He stood outside the ship on the ground and threw a kiss at Sandra as the ship passed by. Sandra knelt on the seat next to the window and cried. He looked at Jadanick his man, The Unpredictable and waved goodbye. The spaceship came back through that place. She saw Jadanick still fighting before the spaceship disappeared into thin skies. Emma heard the spaceship passing through and she ran outside.

"Stop! Stop! Wait for me. You cannot leave me here. Look I can't fight anymore take me with you." She slumped to the ground in despair and started crying. Honestly, she was exhausted. She just wanted to go home.

"Fight or you die. Fight me. You missed the priest. He is one step ahead of you. Look he is still alive," said Jadanick offering Emma a sword.

"You lying monster. How many times must kill me," asked Emma in despair.

"No I am not lying the priest is fighting Alina right now. Look there they are," said Jadanick pointing in the direction where Alina was fighting the priest.

"How is that possible I did exactly like you said," said Emma.

"I don't even know how he did it we have to find out," replied Jadanick.

"Do you still want to kill me, so that we can get even? Here is the sword," said

Jadanick giving the sword to Emma before he knelt in front of her.

"You think I can't do it. Give me that sword," said Emma taking the sword from Jadanick who closed his eyes at first and then just squinted one looking if Emma was going to use the sword on him. She raised the sword and pretended as if to cut Jadanick but she threw the sword at the priest piercing his heart.

"Eh you were saying what priest? What priest were talking about?" asked Emma cunningly. Jadanick got up and looked where the priest and Alina were fighting. The priest was down. He was bleeding through the heart.

"Emma mind your business, will you? Who asked for your help? Now I understand why Jadanick slashed your throat." Jadanick and Alina started laughing.

"What you think this is funny maybe I kill you with my bare hands." Emma ran toward Alina and Alina ran in the opposite direction. The two women chased each other playing cat and mouse while Jadanick was busy laughing at them.

Jadanick walked toward the priest. Pushed the sword deep into the heart to make sure he was dead. He took off the priest's watch and looked at the last person who he had subjugated to.

"No way! That can't be right."

He looked at the ladies and saw them running toward him. He looked behind them. He saw the animals coming their way. The women ran as fast as they can toward Jadanick.

"You wouldn't believe the last person the priest subjugated to," said Jadanick.

"Who was it?" both ladies asked at the same time.

"Jack. Jack was still alive all this time," said Jadanick.

"I guess we have completed our mission. The priest is dead, and we have found the Emperor's wife in Sandra," added Emma.

"One thing I do not understand is that why do we have to die to be used as vessels by the animals. Why can't they just kill the animals and save us to protect the Emperor in the future?" asked Jadanick.

"Unbelievably these animals had been here

for a century and now for them to be reunited with the Emperor in afterlife they need human vessels who can carry them on their tattoos to the next life. So, we must die. To reunite the Emperor with his possessions, we must die for that to happen too," explained Emma.

"Honestly I do not like priests. If they hadn't tricked the Emperor into drowning into the lake, there was no need for him to die and there wouldn't be a need for us to die either," said Alina. What could he have done? There were new threats to the survival of the Emperor. Threats were no longer man. The weather had paused a real threat to the survival of the Emperor. The last Emperor had no heir to continue his bloodline. If he had died and was buried in the place he was supposed to be buried, the weather would have destroyed his DNA. The priests cleverly realized that his DNA will last longer if he is buried underneath the water than on land. The high extreme temperatures meant destruction of his DNA.

"Now we know where to find the Emperor.

Let's go and dig him up and give him a proper burial. Let's get his DNA. Let's search for his bloodline that is if you still want to waste more time. But if you are serious about serving, protecting and honoring the Emperor. Then do as your Emperor asks you to," said Jadanick walking away. The ladies looked at each other and shouted at the same time.

"Jadanick is the Emperor."

They ladies hugged each other and started dancing running toward Jadanick, they all hugged. The animals came too and sat next to them. They believed that Jadanick was the Emperor.

"They do not call me, The Unpredictable for nothing.", said Jadanick looking at his watch and clapping his hands.

"Right on time," he shouted jumping up in the sky clipping his legs in the air. The spaceship with Sandra returned, and he opened the door and said.

"Ladies and animals I present to you, Miss. Sandra, behold the Emperor's future wife." Alina coughed as soon as Jadanick finished saying Emperor's future wife. Jadanick quickly looked at Sandra first and then at Alina before he continued talking. "I mean Emperor's future wife number one. And on your left I present to you, Miss. Alina, behold the Emperor's Magnificent warrior who is also the Emperor's future wife number two by mutual agreement." Emma when she heard this she folded her arms and her lips too. Jadanick quickly looked at her and looked at Sandra and Alina who nodded their heads. Lastly but not least, ladies and animals, I present to you Miss. Emma. The Emperor's Magnificent warrior who is also the Emperor's future wife number three by mutual agreement too.

"Damn! All three! What about us?" whispered the brown lion into the white lion's ears.

"If there is anyone who has reasons why these three beautiful ladies should not be the Emperor's wives please speak now or forever hold your peace," shouted Jadanick.

"Me! Me! Me! Me! Me! Me!" shouted the white lion. The white lion had a crush on

Sandra, so it raised its leg.

"Emperor I could have done exactly what you did with Sandra. I want you to know that I love her very much in fact more than you. I will not in any way send her away in the spaceship alone around the world like some of us did," he paused and looked at the animals who started booing the Emperor.

"Let me continue I have not finished," said the white lion.

"So, that I can spend more time and be with Emma and Alina."

He coughed and said.

"Unlike some of us," looking at the other animals hiding from the Emperor. All the animals started booing the Emperor.

"Silence please! Do you want to end up like the priest? Dead and useless," asked Emma. The white lion continued.

"If you really loved Sandra and wanted to marry Sandra surely if it was me I was never going to kill the only priest who was going to get us wed. In that case I say you are just talk your heart is in love with the twin sisters, Ewalinka and Eva. You are just using Sandra as an excuse."

"Who is Ewalinka and Eva?" asked the Emperor. The white lion remembered Ewalinka and Eva from a century ago. He leaned forward and asked Emma their names.

"I beg your pardon your Highness I meant the twin sister's Emma and Alina," The white lion turned away from the Emperor and talked to the other animals.

"Look at the Emperor's wives that Emma and Alina who do they look like you know?" asked the white lion. All the animals shouted with one voice.

"They all look like Eva and Ewalinka." The white lion went on to address the Emperor.

"I thank you for taking this decision today to marry these ladies. Pardon my French but your father was a fool," said the white lion. The Emperor stood up straight away and shouted at the white lion pointing his fingers at him.

"Do not insult the Emperor my father. My patience is running out with you. Ok?" said the Emperor with an authoritative voice.

"I apologize your Highness. I was just congratulating you. It's better and much wiser for you to marry them than to do like what your father did, killing all of them. I thank you very much. But to conclude I think you made one mistake and because of that I think you do not deserve to marry Sandra. Sandra can never be your wife. She is not the one you love," pleaded the white lion. Jadanick stood up and shouted in anger.

"They are all mine all. All three of them. I love them equally. I love Sandra. I love Emma and I love Alina. You cannot steal from me I am the Emperor," said Jadanick fearing to lose all his wives.

"Now I understand why my father tried to kill all of you," said the Emperor angrily at the animals.

 "Let me finish your Highness," pleaded the white lion.

"You will never leave a scar on the woman you love no matter what. Every woman you should treat her like yours. Never get angry or revenge if there is a woman involved. To make things worse, pardon we animals, but you humans we can never understand you. After you, as you put it yourself, accidental injured her. We heard that you used your tongue to try to choke her too. So, in light of the above, without saying much, I think that, with all due respect, Emperor, you automatically lost your marriage to Sandra and to Emma," said the white lion.

"I ask you White lion, you, cheeky smart-ass. If you were in the shoes of the Emperor, how would you have handled the priest situation," asked Jadanick the Emperor.

"If I really loved these women, first, I would think about them. I would want to marry them first before someone else starts to show interest. The day I heard that you killed the priest I proposed to Sandra. I saw the spaceship going in circles around the globe. I stopped it and I saw a beautiful woman inside and I looked on her fingers she had no ring so I proposed to her. To answer your question, I understand that no man shall kill the Emperor. The priest got your father killed with good intentions," said the white lion. The Emperor rose again.

"Watch what you say about my father. This is the last time I am going to tell you this.", said the Emperor before sitting down. The white lion continued.

"He did not know your father had three wives. He only knew the first wife who died without kids. To preserve your fathers' bloodline, he did what he did. Was it right or wrong? It was wrong but killing the priest is not the answer. To answer your question if it was me I would give the priest a wife." The white lion stopped talking. All the animals saw the funny side of it and started laughing so hard that they felt like their ribs were going to break.

"Do not be daft he is a priest and does not touch women," said Jadanick the Emperor.

"Exactly your Highness that way she will offer him, the priest a ride to heaven...," the white lion did not finish talking as all the other animals started laughing again this time even worse.

"Let me finish. The priest will automatically refuse a ride from the woman you will give him because he should abstain from women. In that case the heavens will automatically deny him excess too to heaven because he will have denied a lift to heaven. So, in the future only the Emperor will go to heaven in afterlife."

They all started clapping hands for the white lion saying that that was great thinking. The Emperor so an opportunity and took it.

"Listen clever white lion. You said you love Sandra and would do anything for her. Right? See, you animals need a vessel to marry a human being, and if you really love Sandra. Enter and use the priest's body," said the Emperor. The lion tried to refuse knowing what was going to happen. The Emperor addressed his wives and the rest of the animals.

"This white lion stood in front of me and insulted my father the great Emperor. He confessed in front of everyone that he will do anything for this woman Sandra. Now I asked him to jump into the only human body or vessel if you want to call it that one of the priest. And now he is trying to refuse," said the Emperor. The white lion jumped into the priest's body and Sandra offered her a ride to heaven. He refused as he was a priest. His ticket to heaven was canceled. As he was never needed in heaven. He could not be reunited with the Emperor in afterlife. The Emperor gave Emma a sword. Emma killed the white lion inside the priest's body.

CHAPTER SIXTEEN

Happily, ever after … ah wait a minute!
"Anymore of you animals who think that I
do not deserve my beautiful three wives
and who think that they should not marry
me, please raise your hand now or forever
keep your peace," asked the Emperor.
"Me!"
"Who said that?" asked the Emperor with
a threatening voice.
"Not you too! What do you want?" asked
Jadanick. Brown lion stood in front of the
Emperor and with a deep, strong voice he
addressed the Emperor.
"I want Emma. She is my better-half. I love

Emma. She is my heart. I will never put a scar on her like you did, and because of that, with all due respect Emperor, you lost Emma," said brown lion.

"They are all mine. These animals trying to steal my wives," said Jadanick hugging all his three women. All the three women stood behind him and said with one voice.

"Emperor address your servant." Jadanick looked at them before addressing the animals.

"I love all these three women please do not make me repeat myself and from this moment in time."

He paused for a little while.

"Law number one. No one shall question the Emperor's private life unless if the Emperor takes what is yours. No one shall take or want what is the Emperor's. So. I ask again. Does anyone here had his 'better-half' taken by the Emperor or among these women," asked Jadanick. No one said anything.

"You, brown lion get out of my sight. Damn! These animals think they can steal my wives and my throne. I told you that no

one is going to steal anything from me."
"No way! I am The Unpredictable."

CHAPTER SEVENTEEN

Fifty years Ago The young Emperor had just turned twenty years old. This was the son of the Emperor Nick which the magnificent seven girls were protecting. His father had died when he was not yet born but still in the womb. No one knew how he died. No one knew the whereabouts of the magnificent seven. The young Emperor had grown up without his parents. No one knew what had happened to his mother either. The temple priests, had sent servants there, to serve and honor him. There were hopes that the magnificent seven were going to be born as in the legend to serve and to honor him. He had waited for these special guards since he learnt about them when he was told about the legend when he turned seven years old himself. At the advice of the priests he had built his Palace underground using his father's fortune. No one knows what the future holds, but the priest had the insight as to what tomorrow would be like.

"So, holy priest where are my holy bodyguards? You said that my father the Emperor had his own holy warriors. Where are mine?" asked young Emperor Brandon. The priest sat down and smoked his pipe before replying.

"Young Emperor, the holy bodyguards, of your father the Emperor, belonged to you too," said the temple priest.

"So, holy priest where are they? You said it yourself that I should have had them at the age of seven years. I am twenty years now. How long more shall I wait. What Emperor can I be without my bodyguards? Why no one tells me about what happened to my father the Emperor? Was he a bad

Emperor?" asked the young Emperor. The temple priest smoked his pipe of herbs. "Young Emperor your father was a great Emperor. All Emperors are great Emperors. I hope and believe that your bodyguards come to you in your days. You see Young Emperor, somehow the rules were broken. We do not know what happened but something bad happened. Your father the Emperor died when he was very young. He didn't even see his 30th birthday. Something terrible must have happened to all his warriors too. It's never heard of. All these centuries magnificent warriors gave Emperor after Emperor a hundred years on earth," explained the priest.

"Am I not an Emperor? Why I do not have the holy warriors. Does that mean I am not worthy protecting?" asked the young Emperor.

"In contrary I think for now there is no danger to you. You see no one knows the Emperor your father had a son you the Emperor. When no one knows, you exist. It means you are safe. No one can look for you to harm you. So, you are safe. The magnificent seven were sent to preserve the Emperor's bloodline and everyone know he died very young and he was not married. In that case, they failed to preserve the bloodline. This has never happened before since the magnificent warriors started protecting the Emperor centuries ago," explained the priest. He looked at the young Emperor and continued.

"Brace yourself young Emperor there shall come evil in the whole land before a new Emperor is anointed again. Whenever the warriors fail and die young they are replaced by the evil warriors who will roam for hundred years too. They say when good fails evil takes over," said the priest looking at the scared young Emperor.

"So, are you saying that I am going to die young like my father the Emperor?" asked the young Emperor looking and feeling sacred.

"No one knows you exist so you shall live like everyone else. No one will look for you to harm you and when time comes the Emperor's bloodline shall be preserved through you. Now it is the responsibilities of the priest to preserve the bloodline. As far as I know no magnificent warriors shall come in your lifetime. But you are still the Emperor," said the priest standing up and walking up and down in front of the young Emperor. The young Emperor at the advice of the priest build an underworld Palace with rooms and everything underground. He stocked all the things he needed and plenty of food. The priest warned him that evil will come looking to clear the earth of the Emperor's bloodline. The young Emperor found his own bodyguards and lived a normal life. After the young Emperor's 22nd birthday the world as we know it changed. Months after the young Emperor's birthday, it was like any other day when the temple priest came to the young Emperor.

"My young Emperor I have seen evil in my dreams. The time has come for you to stay in your underworld Palace until the world has healed," said the priest.

"What happened holy priest?" asked the young Emperor.

"In my dreams, I have seen evil. You are in danger. Go into hiding for some time," replied the priest. The young Emperor made arrangements and stocked food and all the things he needed in his underground Palace. The days and months that came there were reports of people being cooked alive by the sun. There were reports of people being eaten alive. There were reports of people being mauled to death. The ozone layer was destroyed and during the day the sun rays would kill people especially the old. This went on for nearly ten years. After that then came the sudden temperature changes. During the day temperatures were very high and at the night temperature would drop drastically to minus degrees. Each year the situation worsened as day temperatures would rise drastically and at night temperatures would drop drastically quickly forming ice. It took scientists twenty years to figure out what was going on. The ozone layer was being destroyed by gasses and in some parts, had already been destroyed. The scientists then discovered that earth had created another layer to act as a shield, blocking the sun's harmful rays in response to the destruction of the ozone layer. This layer was not far from earth. In the end, they created gates and developed sleeping accommodation and another world there. Over the year's temperature differences between hot and cold has increased and in the end, it was impossible to sleep on earth. At night temperatures, would plummet to below freezing. During the day, the world above was inhabitable as there was no protection above from the direct ultraviolet harmful sun's rays. In the end, everyone ended up with two accommodation one up the new world and one on earth. This huge temperature difference created a big problem for everyone especially the priests. Their role was to preserve the bloodline of the Emperor. They were to look after the young Emperor until he had died. There were going to bury him per their tradition and perform the ritual needed to safeguard the continuation of the birth of the magnificent seven. The young Emperor is now in his late forties. The biggest problem is the daily commute to the above world to sleep. The original priest was old and commuting every day was a challenge. The Emperor had no money. He had used all his father's fortune building and provide energy to keep warmth at night. Only the priest would know what to do if the Emperor dies today. And only the priest would be able to communicate that message in the trance or dreams for future generations. Some servants and bodyguards of the former young Emperor started dying of cold and losing limbs as they adamantly refused to leave the Emperor's Palace. The Emperor in the first days stayed in his Palace with his servants and bodyguards. He braced the cold nights day after day. In the end, he had no money. The priest woke up one day and sat down. He thought and thought. In the end, he got up, in his old age and walked out of the city alone. The whole day he was out alone. When he came back, he spoke to the Emperor, and he went to sleep. In the morning, he woke up and spoke to the Emperor.

"Emperor, I had a dream. There is another place where earth is habitable at night. A place where you will be able to live in peace and for a long time. A place where in the end you will have the magnificent warriors. A ship will come to take us there," he paused for a while. The Emperor had no money. All his servants and bodyguards were dying night after night. He had refused to commute daily to the new world above. This was the best option he had. On hearing this, he was delighted.

"Holy one at last the gods have answered our prayers. Earth has become hostile to her kids. Humankind no long inhabit earth at night. The gods have forsaken us. Why can't they send the magnificent warriors to save us? Now we need their help," said the Emperor pleading with the priest.

"I know the gods work in mysterious ways and this is the answer. They will send a ship to take us to a land where we will be able to see the magnificent warriors again.

Once we are there, they will surely grant us these delightful warriors. We shall never mourn one of us every day again. They shall send us the sun to warm us when we are cold. This will only be possible if we go to the ship and leave this bewitched land," explained the priest.

"So, where we board this ship?" asked the Emperor hopefully. The priest waited for a while. He coughed for some time and smoked his pipe.

"Emperor there is a lake outside of the city and the ship shall come there," he stopped talking and coughed again. He was now very old. The Emperor put his arms around him.

"Holy one be strong now the gods have rescued us. We shall go to the lake but why the lake if I may ask? Why not here? Outside the Palace. You can't walk all the way there, Holy priest?" asked the Emperor. The priest had no answer to that, he paused and quickly put the pipe in his mouth thinking.

"The waters of the lake. The ship can easily land there than anywhere here. We do not want it to get damaged. We want to go to this new land. Would you not agree Emperor?" asked the priest.

"Sure, I agree. We shall go when the time comes," said the Emperor.

"When the day arrived, I will tell you we shall go you and your son and your wife only," said the priest looking at the Emperor.

"What about the rest? Most had stayed here with me all their lives. I can't leave them here alone? We must go with them," said the Emperor seriously.

"I know Emperor. The ship shall return for all of them once you are safe," replied the priest. Since this day, the priest stayed in his room most of the days reciting his prayers. He would talk to the Emperor here and there but not as much as he used to do. Days passed by without any news about the ship.

"Any news about the ship," asked the Emperor.

"Not yet I have not received any messages yet. I have been praying constantly," replied the priest. Weeks after this most of the Emperor's bodyguards and servants had died. He was now fearing for the death of his family. His money was running out. He had no option. He had to go to the ship and go to another land where earth was habitable at night. Weeks after the priest came to the Emperor to talk.

"Emperor it's time I had a dream. The ship is coming tonight. We will all go tonight your family and me. So, get ready," said the priest.

"At last the gods have answered our prayers.", remarked the Emperor. He was happy that day. He spoke to the remaining servants and bodyguards assuring them that the ship will come for them. The same to his bodyguards.

"Are you ready it's night time we have to go?" asked the priest.

"Yes, priest we are all ready," replied the Emperor. They went to the lake. By the time, they arrived there outside had started to be very cold. They arrive at the lake and the priest quickly indicated that the ship was inside the lake so he had to get it out. He quickly jumped into the lake and disappeared underneath the water. Minutes later he resurfaced.

"I can't get it out. Its wedge under logs and I am an old man now. If it was some years ago, I could have done it by myself. I am afraid I will need your help. Just leave your wife on the shore. If we go both into the water, we will be out in no time," said the priest.

"Wait here we will be out soon. Do not get into the water. The water is too cold for you," said the Emperor talking to his wife.

"No. Please Emperor do not go wait here outside. Please do not go.", said the Emperor's wife feeling like crying.

"Please do not leave us," added the Emperor's wife.

"I am not leaving you. We are just going down to locate the ship and we will be out in no town."

"Are you ready?" asked the priest.

"Yes. We are.", replied the Emperor. The Emperor and his son braced the cold waters. They stood on the edge of the lake waters waiting for the priest's signal.

"Oh by the way when we are in the water

we have to go deep down quickly to the bottom of the lake and lift the ship up," said the priest. The Emperor's son jumped into the lake.

"We do not have time," shouted the priest. "Emperor do not go," said the Emperor's wife with a soft voice. The Emperor stood there without saying anything and looked at his wife before jumping into the lake waters.

"Straight to the lake bottom," shouted the priest. The three man went right at the bottom of the lake. The Emperor looked under his feet and saw green stones glowing. He was standing on the stones. Soon afterward he started looking around for the ship. He was about to swim to the other side when he went into a trance and fainted. The priest too stood on the green stones and went into a trance. His son tried to lift his father and resurface but tragedy struck. As soon as he touched his father the Emperor, the Emperor's son went into a trance too. The Emperor's wife waited and waited but no one came out. The weather was changing rapidly. She knew that there was nothing she could have done. She only had to serve herself and she started going back before temperatures change drastically. She shouted the Emperor's name maybe a hundred times before she started going back. She would walk a few feet and then look backward to see if anyone was coming out of the lake. She went straight back and went up to the world above. The three man perished within minutes in the freezing waters of the lake. Months later the Emperor's wife was found mauled to death by an animal.

****

THE END

www.ingramcontent.com/pod-product-compliance
Lightning Source LLC
Chambersburg PA
CBHW032102180726
48284CB00002B/400